Lord Ruthven
Begins

LORD RUTHVEN BEGINS

BEGINS

(*Douglas the Vampire*)

by
Jules Dornay

adapted in English by
Frank J. Morlock

A Black Coat Press Book

This play is dedicated to my good friend, Tony Smith.
FJM

Visit our website at www.blackcoatpress.com

ISBN 978-1-935558-43-9. First Printing. November 2010.
Published by Black Coat Press, an imprint of Hollywood
Comics.com, LLC, P.O. Box 17270, Encino, CA 91416. All
rights reserved. Except for review purposes, no part of this
book may be reproduced or transmitted in any form or by any
means, electronic or mechanical, including photocopying,
recording, or by any information storage and retrieval system,
without permission in writing from the publisher. The stories
and characters depicted in this book are entirely fictional.
Printed in the United States of America.

Table of Contents

Introduction

Douglas le Vampyre, translated here as *Lord Ruth-ven Begins*, was first presented at the Théâtre Beaumarchais in Paris on August 13, 1865.

Douglas was but the most recent in a series of novels, stories and plays exploiting the myth of the vampire, introduced with great success in 1819 by John William Polidori in his short story *The Vampyre*. The tale was falsely attributed to Lord Byron when it first appeared, which no doubt only increased its appeal.

The Vampyre proved enormously successful and was immediately copied by Cyprien Bérard, who authored *Lord Rutwen ou les Vampires* in 1820, which was then promptly adapted into a stage play by Charles Nodier the same year. Nodier's play, and another 1821 short vaudeville entitled *Le Vampire* by the well-known libretto writer Eugène Scribe also featuring Ruthven, are available in the Black Coat press collection *Lord Ruthven the Vampire*.[1]

The vampire, which had previously been mocked by Voltaire in his *Dictionnaire Philosophique* (1764), had suddenly become a Byronesque romantic icon, taking the literary establishment by storm.

In 1823, the Théâtre de la Gaîté in Paris featured a play entitled *Polichinelle Vampire*. In 1825, in a three-volume novel simply entitled *La Vampire*, Étienne-Léon de Lamothe-Langon told the story of a young Napoleonic army officer who brought his Hungarian fiancée back home to later discover that she was, in reality, a vampire.

---

[1] ISBN 1-932983-10-4.

Even Prosper Mérimée's *La Guzla* (1827), a literary hoax comprised of ballads about murder, revenge and vampires, allegedly translated from the Illyrian by "Hiacynthe Maglanowich," included a pseudo-academic study of vampirism!

Théophile Gautier's *La Morte Amoureuse* [The Loving Dead] (1836) was a breakthrough in vampire fiction, being a precursor to modern-day romantic vampire novels by Chelsea Quinn Yarbro and Ann Rice. Its vampire is not a soulless creature of the night like Lamothe-Langon's female Ruthven, but a loving, sensitive and beautiful woman, who inspires a strong romantic passion in the heart of a young priest, who is eventually forced by his superiors to slay her.

Alexandre Dumas, a writer gifted with a prodigious imagination and a born storyteller, was finely attuned to the trends and fashions of the marketplace. The success of Hoffmann's *Tales* influenced him to write *Les Mille et Un Fantômes* [A Thousand and One Ghosts] (1849), an anthology of macabre tales, linked by the now-classic device of guests sharing ghostly tales at a dinner party. Among its contents was a story about a vampire who preyed on a girl and was eventually destroyed by being nailed in his coffin with a consecrated sword. Dumas returned to the theme with the more elaborate *Le Vampire* (1851), which featured the return of the indomitable Lord Ruthven, this time clashing with a female ghoul endowed with magical powers. *Le Vampire* is available in a Black Coat Press edition under the title *The Return of Lord Ruthven*.[2]

Pierre-Alexis Ponson du Terrail, the creator of Rocambole, also dabbled in vampire fiction with *La Ba-*

[2] ISBN 1-932983-11-2.

ronne Trépassée, in which the hero's dead wife returns as a female vampire in the service of the legendary Black Huntsman of Bohemia. The novel is available in a Black Coat Press edition as *The Vampire and the Devil's Son*.[3]

Le Vampire du Val-de-Grâce (1861) by Léon Gozlan is a mere pot-boiler; far more interesting are Paul Féval's *La Vampire* (1856) and *Le Chevalier Ténèbre* (1862). The first novel is about a perversely charismatic female vampire who preys on humans, not just for blood, but for money as well; the second relates the criminal exploits of two vampire brothers across Europe—or are they mere conmen? Both novels play with all the archetypes of the genre, and create new ones as well. *La Vampire* and *Le Chevalier Ténèbre* are available in Black Coat Press editions respectively as *The Vampire Countess* and *Knightshade*.[4]

Which brings us to *Douglas le Vampyre*, written in 1865, only a few years after the aforementioned works. Unlike Féval's or Gautier's works, Dornay's play is not ground-breaking but unashamedly popular, making good use of the traditional vampire elements previously set up by Dumas and, before him, Nodier and Polidori. This is why, without making any other changes to the play, it was easy to rechristen its eponymous protagonist "Ruthven," because in terms of looks, motivations and actions, Lord Douglas is but the handsome, predatory Lord Ruthven under another guise.

Jules Dornay was born in Blois on March 13, 1835. He was, in his day, a prolific and highly successful dramatist, not unlike a top television writer today. His spe-

---

[3] ISBN 1-932983-55-4.
[4] ISBNs 0-9740711-5-3 and 0-9740711-4-5.

cialty was adapting other writers' works to the stage. He began his career in the theater as an actor, but left the stage in 1859 to write plays, sometimes three in the same year. *Douglas le Vampyre* was, in fact, one of his few "original" (using the word loosely) works. His credits include *La Lionne de la Place Maubert* (1860), *L'Homme au Masque Rouge* (1861), *Les Hirondelles du Pont d'Arcole* (with Eugène Moreau) (1861), *Les Fantômes de la Chambre Rouge* (with Deslandes) (1963), *Le Cabaret de la Grappe Dorée* (with Moreau) (1865), *Les Vendanges du Clos-Tavannes* (with Moreau) (1865), *Jean Raisin* (with Maurice Coste) (1876), *Gavroche* (avec Lange) (1888), and a slew of adaptations of Xavier Aymon de Montepin, including *Lantara* (1865), *Les Cocodès* (1865), *L'Homme aux Figures de Cire* (1865), *Bas-de-cuir* (1866), *Le Roi de la Lune*, *La Marchande de Fleurs*, *La Policière* (1889) and *La Porteuse de Pain* (1889), a melodrama which has been filmed half-a-dozen times, first in 1916 and last in 1973, for French television.

Dornay was very active in the world of Parisian theater and, at one time, even managed a troupe at the Théâtre de l'Ambigu. That such a successful author left so few literary memories today—he is not even listed in Larousse's Dictionary of Authors!—is a testimony to the ephemeral nature of commercial success. *Sic transit gloria mundi!*

Jean-Marc Lofficier

Lord Ruthven Begins

Characters

Lord Ruthven, The Vampire
Reginald
The Sheriff
Tom Platt
Dick Thorn
Fanny
Maxwell
Anna Clifford
Sir William Clifford
Betsy
Hurley
Aunt Sarah
Allison
First Guest
Second Guest
First Lady
Second Lady
First Sailor
Second Sailor
Third Sailor
A Peasant
Lords, Guests, Pages, Seamen, Peasants, Scots, Ladies
and Peasant Women

The action takes place in Edinburgh and its suburbs in
1648.

ACT I

Scene I

A large lit-up garden. Massive trees and shrubbery. Statues and marble benches in the rear and in perspective. The wing of a castle where windows are brilliantly lit.

AT RISE, the garden is full of guests strolling about in groups, wearing different sorts of costumes. Some are masked.

A group of young people enter and surround the Sheriff.

REGINALD
(to the young people)
Ah, ah, you've abandoned the game room, gentlemen.

FIRST GUEST
It was suffocating in that room.

REGINALD
Still, the parties ought to be interesting. Isn't that so, Sheriff?

SHERIFF
Yes, Sir William Clifford was making a hellish gamble. If the direction he's heading in doesn't change, he runs the risk of leaving a large portion of his estate on the gaming table.

REGINALD

What does he care! Doesn't he expect the inheritance of Lord Ruthven?

SHERIFF

He hopes!

REGINALD

Well, they say with reason...

SECOND GUEST

Do you think so?

REGINALD

I believe that he's the only serious heir to the fortune of the Ruthvens. And he himself is so certain of it that, for the last four months, he's placed his house on a footing of exceptional luxury, parties, games, masquerades.

FIRST GUEST

Still, isn't there talk of an unknown heir?

REGINALD

Yes, a grandson of Ruthven.

SHERIFF

Whose existence is no less certain and who for the first inheritance reaped the rumor of the anger of the deceased against his daughter.

REGINALD

Oh, Lord Sheriff, say rather against her marriage for love.

SHERIFF

He was right, gentlemen. Lucy Ruthven had justified her father's severity by a secret marriage, an elopement to Moldavia, I think, the country of the husband she'd chosen.

REGINALD

Time didn't lead to any change in the Puritan temperament of her father?

SHERIFF

No, the birth of a child only increased his fury. All attempts at reconciliation were brutally rejected.

REGINALD

Yet there's every reason to believe Lord Ruthven has repented.

SHERIFF

To suppose it, perhaps—admitting that emissaries sent by him to Germany had for their mission to find that child.

REGINALD

Who must be a man today.

SHERIFF

And who has nonetheless vanished since the death of his parents. Old Ruthven himself died two months ago without knowing to whom he was leaving his immense domains, his titles and his name.

FIRST GUEST

In that case, why hasn't Sir William taken possession of his inheritance already?

SHERIFF

Because the deceased prolonged the suspense by delaying the reading of his will until two months after his death. Tomorrow at noon, the will shall be read.

REGINALD

That delay was made, no question, with his wish for a grandson in mind.

SHERIFF

Of course, but it was a useless precaution in my view. If the grandson is not here tonight, he won't be here tomorrow.

REGINALD

Sir William is less confident than you, Sheriff. His feverish gambling proves that.

SHERIFF

His role is more interested than mine.

REGINALD

Whoever the heir, the expenses remain the same.

SHERIFF
(gaily)

And will be no less discharged. The tax collector never comes off the worse.

They go off chatting.

Tom Platt enters, looking behind him.

TOM PLATT
Now those are candles! These lights prevent me from seeing clearly!
(jostling a lady)
Ah, excuse me, Madam! I was dazzled.

Dick Thorn enters. Tom Platt bumps into him.

TOM PLATT
Ah, pardon me, gentle sir, I didn't see you.

DICK THORN
Look down and you will see me. 'Sdeath!

TOM PLATT
(aside)
Now here's one who isn't gracious.

DICK THORN
(speaking to his sword)
Ah, Virginia, my beauty, I didn't think I'd have the pleasure of making your blade sparkle beneath the stars tonight. Don't be too bored, my angel! Do like me, take time as it comes, but always hope.

TOM PLATT
Where will I find my new master? He's still recognizable...
(to Dick Thorn)
Pardon, Milord, have you seen a man wearing a red-jacket?

DICK THORN
I've seen thirty-two. Which one do you want?

TOM PLATT
(aside)
Decidedly, not gracious.

Tom moves away and becomes lost in the crowd.

DICK THORN
(watching him go)
If I'm not mistaken, I've seen those shoulders under the livery of the late Lord Ruthven. Could the Baronet have taken you into his service already? He's stealing from the heir. You should hold off, Sir William; tomorrow is not today.

Dick moves away and vanishes in the crowd.

Reginald returns with Fanny and Maxwell, who are wearing masks.

REGINALD
What, my dear Fanny? You, shocked by such a small thing?

Fanny unmasks and sits down.

FANNY
That man doesn't frighten me, Reginald. But what I experienced in seeing him is impossible to describe.

Maxwell unmasks too.

MAXWELL

Fanny's right. I myself shivered when my glance met that of this singular character.

FIRST LADY (masked)

You are speaking, aren't you, Doctor, of that man who, beneath his diabolic costume, wears a large red jacket?

SECOND LADY

The "Wraith," as they are already calling him.

MAXWELL

Yes, Miladies.

FIRST LADY

I feel just like you; his appearance in the midst of this party has produced a most uncomfortable impression on us.

FANNY

There's nothing human about his face. And yet his eyes… This pallor terrifies and captivates at the same time.

FIRST LADY

Hold on. Here he is!

At this moment, the so-called "Wraith" appears at the rear, looks about, then vanishes. The Sheriff enters behind him.

SECOND LADY

Oh, I'm quivering despite myself.

FANNY

What about his slow pace? One would swear it's a corpse emerging from the tomb.

MAXWELL

How to explain such a phenomenon? It's pointless for us to seek reasons for such pallor. Science doesn't know yet how to answer our questions...

REGINALD

Let's not try then. He's a very pale gentleman, that's all. Does anyone know his name?

SHERIFF

How would one know it? Sir William has opened his house to foreigners passing through Edinburgh. He presented himself, he was allowed to enter, and here he is.

REGINALD

Still we know he's a foreigner. He displeases us. Would you like me to tell him? He might get angry. Then we will pull out our swords...

FANNY

Reginald!

REGINALD

I'm joking.

FIRST GUEST

If there was dirty work there to be done... Hold on! Here is a man who'd be ready to do it.
                    (pointing to Dick Thorn who passes at the back)

FANNY

That man?

MAXWELL

Dick Thorn.

FIRST GUEST

Do you know him?

SHERIFF

Who doesn't know him? Why has Sir William put us in the position of rubbing elbows with a fellow like that?

DICK THORN
(aside, passing)

Sir William has left the gaming table. Where the Devil has he got to?

REGINALD

Everything is weird here tonight. Who's this Dick Thorn character?

SHERIFF

One of Sir William's cousins! A bravo at the service of whoever pays him. A downright bandit who seeks to enthrone the customs of Italy in the highlands of Scotland. He provokes and kills, but always cleverly enough so that the law sees only a regular duel, where the Devil smells out an assassination. In my capacity as Sheriff, I'm obliged to be aware of his presence here.

REGINALD

He kills for money?

SHERIFF

Or so they say. Men talk; the Sheriff doesn't swear to it.

REGINALD

Let's take up a collection then, gentlemen.

FIRST GUEST

Why?

REGINALD

So as to have a sum to give him if he'll rid us of that Wraith.

SHERIFF

Or perhaps that Wraith will rid us of him.

REGINALD

Whatever the outcome it's worth something.

MAXWELL

The simplest thing would be to leave the two of them alone.

The guests slowly move away leaving only Reginald, Fanny and Maxwell on stage.

REGINALD

What's wrong with Maxwell this evening? He's so sad.

FANNY

He's always like that every time he approaches Anna. And yet, Anna loves him, I'm sure of it.

REGINALD

Who couldn't help but loving him?

FANNY

Sir William Clifford!

REGINALD

Come on, will you. Maxwell is a scientist.

FANNY

Science is all he has.

REGINALD

It's a fortune, too. Counting that way, he's as rich as Sir William. And that's not an obstacle that can shackle his ambition, his desires…

FANNY

Oh, you're wrong about that.

REGINALD

Let Maxwell speak to Anna's father, and you will see, he'll be as fortunate as I am

Anna Clifford appears at rear, masked; she listens.

FANNY

My brother loves you, Reginald. He's not ambitious for himself or for me, whereas Anna's father is not thinking of the happiness of his daughter.

REGINALD

Yes, your brother and I both want you to be happy, and for my part…

FANNY:

Darling...

ANNA
(who's heard the conversation, leaning between
Reginald and Fanny, unmasking)
Both of them.

FANNY

Anna! My dear Anna!

REGINALD
(bowing)
Miss Clifford! You've made this party wait for your gracious presence. That's bad.

ANNA
(offering him her hand)
An ill passage. You'll forgive me.

REGINALD
(kissing her hand)
I forgive you , provided you ask a Doctor for a consultation over this ill passage.
(pointing to Maxwell seated, dreaming)

ANNA

Maxwell!

FANNY
(pointing to Maxwell)
It's by loving him that you will bring about my happiness.

ANNA

By loving him. Doesn't he have all my thoughts? Why doesn't he ask Sir William, and say to him, "You are her father, be mine as well."

FANNY

But what if Sir William rejected him?

ANNA

Rejected him!

FANNY

Come, let's tear him from his dreaming.

They go towards Maxwell, chatting,

REGINALD
(looking at Maxwell)

O man! What an atom you become in the presence of love! Look what love has made of this formidable hero of science: a dreamer dying of despair. O weakness of the stronger sex!

FANNY
(going to Maxwell)

Maxwell!

ANNA

Good evening, Maxwell. Have courage! I have only one thing to say to you: go and talk to my father.

MAXWELL

Yes, yes, this evening. Oh, I'll dare all for you to be my wife!

Sir William Clifford enters in the midst of another group of strollers.

ANNA
(seeing her father)
My father…

MAXWELL
(aside)
Will I find sufficient courage?

SIR WILLIAM
(to the ladies)
Well, Miladies, you are neglecting the ball. Gentlemen, be worthy guests, leave nothing to desire!
(seeing Maxwell)
Ah, it's you, Doctor!

MAXWELL
(bowing)
Sir William.

SIR WILLIAM
(dryly)
How is it that we have the happy fortune of being your host tonight. What tears you from your serious studies?

ANNA
(aside)
Such frigidity!

SIR WILLIAM
The pleasures of the great are scorned by men who grow pale over scientific books. They treat as folly these hap-

py meetings until, one day, the hope of sharing them comes into their hearts, either furtively or through marriage...

FANNY
(aside)
My God!

REGINALD
(aside)
What arrogance!

SIR WILLIAM
...But you are not one of those, Doctor. You are right. Study. Work We are the fools, you are the sage.

MAXWELL
The fools are the sages, Milord!

SIR WILLIAM
Miss Fanny, your brother's preoccupations don't concern you. Enjoy the ball, and don't resist the seductions of pleasure.

Sir William loses himself in the groups of partiers.

FANNY
(to Anna)
How Maxwell must suffer.

REGINALD
(to Maxwell)
He put you in despair, didn't he?

MAXWELL

Those frigid words fell on my heart like drops of ice water. Does he suspect my love?

REGINALD

You're exaggerating. It's just his self aggrandizing pride.

MAXWELL

That pride even shocks me. There's where the danger lies.

REGINALD

No reason to fear it, until you know the danger exists.

MAXWELL

Ah, I was right to say wise men are fools. A man is nothing if he is neither rich nor noble. Wise men are allowed to be ambitious but not happy.
(collapsing on a bench)
You are a scientist? You are famous? That's not enough for you? You are not a man like other men. There's the money, you've been paid. Don't ask for more.

REGINALD

Maxwell! Courage!

MAXWELL

What's the use?

REGINALD

Do you no longer love her?

MAXWELL

Not love her? You're right... Yes, I'll speak to him.

Sir William returns and looks around.

SIR WILLIAM
(aside)
He resembles Lucy Ruthven. It's him, it must be him—
and ruin follows.

Maxwell goes to speak to Sir William, while Anna and
Fanny appear at the left.

MAXWELL

Baronet…

SIR WILLIAM

Doctor!

MAXWELL
(to Anna and Fanny)
Don't go away, Miss Clifford, sister, please stay.

SIR WILLIAM

All this agitation. What's going on?

MAXWELL

Nothing to be frightened about. I have two questions for
you.

SIR WILLIAM

For me?

MAXWELL

Yes.

SIR WILLIAM

Please explain yourself, doctor.

ANNA
(to Fanny)

I'm shaking.

FANNY

My poor brother!

MAXWELL

Do you respect science, Sir William?

SIR WILLIAM

Certainly, I respect it.

MAXWELL

Enough to offer it a hand in some circumstance, whatever they may be.

SIR WILLIAM

In some circumstances, yes. I've given you proof of it, Doctor, as well as to others.

MAXWELL

Thank you for those words, Sir William; they encourage me. You think me a scientist, you treat me as such...

SIR WILLIAM

Your presence here tonight is proof of it.

MAXWELL

Well then—if a scientist such as myself, for example, dared to aspire to a young girl's hand, your daughter for example, dared to dream that one day she might become his wife, and he came to tell you so, how would you reply to him?

ANNA
(aside)
My God!

SIR WILLIAM
(after a moment of silence)
How ill chosen this moment is to broach a question like this. My daughter's destiny cannot be the object of an unconsidered reply...
(he moves away and sits down)

MAXWELL

But you haven't said no.

SIR WILLIAM

I will consider it, Doctor, I will consider it.

MAXWELL

You leave me a bit of hope, Sir William, and I thank you.

MAXWELL
(to Anna)
My cause is in now your hands, Miss Clifford.

ANNA

I will speak to my father tonight, after the ball.

MAXWELL
(to Anna)
Allow me to escort you into the salons.

ANNA
Come.

They distance themselves slowly to the right.

FANNY
(to Reginald)
How happy Maxwell is.

REGINALD
The Baronet spoke too long about it. A single word: "yes" would have sufficed.

They leave behind Maxwell.

SIR WILLIAM
(aside)
Tomorrow, Baronet Sir William Clifford will become Lord William Ruthven, and all the scientists in the country cannot bridge the distance that will separate you from my daughter. Tomorrow.
(rising)
Tomorrow is too slow coming. And the closer I get to the appointed hour, the more fearful I become. That Wraith. Who is he? If he is the son of Lucy Ruthven, what remains of all my hopes, all my dreams, all my ambitions? Nothing! Only the unbearable mediocrity in which my life has unfolded for fifty years. No, no! No man shall take this dazzling future from me…

SIR WILLIAM (cont'd)

Whoever he may be, this man excites my fears. That suffices. He must disappear!

Dick Thorn enters from the right.

DICK THORN

Gambling's a silly thing when you cannot take part.

SIR WILLIAM
(noticing him)

Captain Dick Thorn. It's not mere chance that brings him to me at this hour.

DICK THORN

Why, it's you Sir William! Sitting here all by yourself, the director of so much pleasure seems to disdain it.

SIR WILLIAM

At my age, the ball doesn't offer any attraction.

DICK THORN

That's true. Your face is careworn. Is it about the Ruthven inheritance?

SIR WILLIAM

Yes, I've been poor for so long.

DICK THORN

I've been Captain Jab too long myself.

SIR WILLIAM

I understand you. You like gambling?

DICK THORN

Gambling! It's joy.

SIR WILLIAM

Women?

DICK THORN

Another joy.

SIR WILLIAM

Wine?

DICK THORN

Yet another joy.

SIR WILLIAM

Dueling perhaps?

DICK THORN

Ah, no! Not me. But Virginia here…
          (placing his hand on the hilt of his sword)
…she's devilishly sensitive. For a cross-eyed look, she dances in her scabbard; for a gesture, she leaves it; for a word, she bursts into flame.

SIR WILLIAM
          (low)
And for how much does she kill?

DICK THORN
          (standing straight up)
What? Sir William, if anyone else addressed this insult to me…

SIR WILLIAM
Then it's not true?

DICK THORN
(changing his tone)

On my way sometimes, I've met some highly nervous temperaments for whom the duel is objectionable, but who, nonetheless, resent an insult or offense. By nature, I am an obliging man. So I unsheathe Victoria for them! In return, on my behalf, they repair the injustices of fortune. An exchange of gallant dealings. Am I a bravo for that?

SIR WILLIAM
No, certainly not. In my opinion at least. Not everyone would share it, of course.

DICK THORN
Who would dare say otherwise?

SIR WILLIAM
No one between you and me. Your fellow citizens know you and appreciate you…

DICK THORN
Excellent.

SIR WILLIAM
…But you've traveled a lot, Dick…

DICK THORN
Yes, I have—perfecting my education as a gentleman, you might say.

SIR WILLIAM

...And as you were on a short vacation, they slandered you. Instead of an obliging knight errant, they've depicted you as an ordinary mercenary.

DICK THORN

Truly?

SIR WILLIAM

At least, that's what they insinuate.

DICK THORN

In that case, who? A name! I want a name!
(to his sword)
Virginia, be calm.

SIR WILLIAM

I don't know exactly. A foreigner. Some Moldavian Count.

DICK THORN

Ah! The man with the red jacket?

SIR WILLIAM

Yes. I cannot swear to it exactly, but it seemed to me...

DICK THORN
(after a pause)
Sir William...

SIR WILLIAM

Captain Thorn?

DICK THORN

Are we no longer friends?

SIR WILLIAM

What does that question mean?

DICK THORN

What's the use of so many dodges? Speak to me frankly.

SIR WILLIAM

Very well. The succession of Lord Ruthven is not yet in my hands. The heir who could deprive me of it is expected from Moldavia. There's a face, tonight, amongst all these guests—a face which worries me, and that I'd gladly rid myself of...

DICK THORN

Come on, dear Baronet, be precise. Don't seek to make me take the quarrel on my own behalf. Tell me, instead....

SIR WILLIAM
(low, and in a dry tone)

Dick, I need you.

DICK THORN

Fine. Only it's no longer me, it's Virginia who must address you.
(pulling his sword)
Virginia, my beauty, leave your hiding place, coquette, and reply. Are you ready to fight for Sir William Clifford? Ha ha! The gallant lady really wants to. You are one of her friends, you see. And do you answer for victory? She nods, the boastful slut. Huh? What?

DICK THORN (cont'd)

The reward? Ah, cousin, you said it yourself, it's her reputation. Virginia is very selfish. Nothing for nothing.

SIR WILLIAM

The reward? Name it yourself.

DICK THORN
(questioning his sword, tapping his fingers on
the blade, then touching his ear)
Huh? Oh, that's rather small! Still!
(aloud to Clifford)
A thousand pounds

SIR WILLIAM
(aghast)
A thousand pounds?

DICK THORN

It's not my price, it's Virginia's. Don't bargain with her, it's useless, she doesn't like it. She'll go back into hiding, and nothing, not even my prayers, will get her to come out.
(putting his sword back in his scabbard)

SIR WILLIAM

Well, that's agreed. But you'll need a pretext.

DICK THORN

Oh, that's not a difficulty. Give me a few gold pieces on account. I'll play against him. I'll lose. Then I'll accuse him of cheating. Better yet, I'll get myself accused, and that will be more credible. And I'll have more justification.

SIR WILLIAM
(giving him a purse)
An absurd trick...

DICK THORN
The important thing is that it works! I might find another, perhaps. Because I am going to put blood in his face.

Reginald and Maxwell return.

REGINALD
If it's that fellow from Moldavia you're speaking of, I warn you...

DICK THORN
Why's that, Mr. Reginald!

REGINALD
...Because he's like a marble statue, a ghost, a spectre, whatever you like, but not a man. Men alone have blood in their veins.

DICK THORN
In your place I'd say right away that he's a vampire.

Suddenly all the partiers stop and gather closer.

ALL
A vampire!

SHERIFF
What's that?

REGINALD
(laughing)
By Jove, don't you get it? The man with the pale face
and the red jacket is a vampire.

ALL

A vampire!

TOM PLATT
(aside)
My master—a vampire? Brr!

MAXWELL
Don't joke, Reginald. And don't deny the existence of
the undead.

SIR WILLIAM
Do you believe in them, Doctor?

MAXWELL
I don't dare believe in them, and yet, the books of our
predecessors speak of them with so much certainty that,
from time to time, I am tempted to bow to their convic-
tion.

REGINALD
You make me laugh.

The pale-faced stranger appears at the back, listening.

MAXWELL
Not at all. There are many accounts going back even to
Homer…

MAXWELL (cont'd)

The *Lamia*, translated by Saint Jerome, gives us terrible details of these maleficent creatures who, like hyenas, live only from the cadavers they've disinterred.

ALL

Ah!

DICK THORN
(aside)

If he's a dead man, Virginia shouldn't have much trouble.

MAXWELL

The Slav, Greek, and Romanian populations of the principalities of the Danube, Greece, Hungary, Poland all report this superstition, and who knows if there's not a grain of truth in these tales.

ALL

A grain of truth!

SHERIFF

You are terrifying, Doctor Maxwell.

STRANGER
(coming closer)

Doctor Maxwell's right, gentlemen.

ANNA
(to Fanny)

That man freezes my blood!

STRANGER

Right or wrong, vampirism is a belief in the countries which the Doctor named.

REGINALD

(low, to Maxwell, looking at the stranger)

What a strange physiognomy…

MAXWELL

(low to Reginald)

His voice is not of this world.

STRANGER

You have to believe it a little.

REGINALD

(going to him)

Do you actually believe it, sir?

STRANGER

Why not?

ALL

Ah!

REGINALD

But what kind of spirits are these "vampires?"

STRANGER

Not spirits at all, but bodies whose privilege it is not to decompose in the earth, however damp or hot it may be. With them, all sources of life have not been exhausted. They feed on human blood.

ANNA

On blood!

STRANGER

Which they extract from the veins of sleeping people, especially young virgins.

ANNA

That's horrible.

STRANGER

At the hour of midnight, the Vampire rushes from his tomb; he gorges himself on the blood of his sleeping victims, eagerly; but the same blood oozes through all his pores, and spreads on his path, leaving a clear trail to his tomb or his ditch! Then, when the living are able to surprise him, they forcefully shove a stake into his breast, and slice off his head—his mouth uttering a horrible scream in the process. Then, they throw the head and cadaver into the flames. Once reduced to ashes, the Vampire enters into the communal and silent condition of the ordinary dead and ceases to trouble the repose of the living forever.

REGINALD

Enough, you are scaring the ladies!

STRANGER

I was merely detailing the Doctor's legend, Miladies, but this gentleman is correct; this story has no place at a costume ball, and I'll say no more about it. It's delirium and fear that cradles these terrifying monsters.

MAXWELL

Perhaps.

TOM PLATT
(aside)
I guess I'm stuck with him...

STRANGER

If terror has gripped your souls, don't hold it against me, ladies. Doctor Maxwell gave the tune, I've simply been chanting off this lugubrious ballad...

Music is heard.

STRANGER (cont'd)

...And—hold on! By good luck, the violins of Sir William Clifford are changing the theme, and now, they cast their joyful notes to the winds, as if to tell you that there's nothing real here—except pleasure.

REGINALD
(aside)
His joy seems a bit forced.

All the company moves away talking. The guests disappear.

SIR WILLIAM
(to Dick Thorn)
So what have you decided?

DICK THORN

I've got what I need. He's a dead man. Virginia is filled with excitement.

They step back.

> STRANGER
> (looking at Anna and Fanny
> who move away)

Those two young girls are quite beautiful If I must choose between them…

> TOM PLATT

I feel vampirized. It's as if I no longer have a drop of blood in my veins.

Tom leaves.

> STRANGER

Their beauty has something fatal in it.

Dick Thorn approaches him.

> DICK THORN

Sir, I had never believed in the existence of vampires.

> STRANGER
> (looking at him coldly)

Really?

> DICK THORN

Yes. I had always regarded them as fabulous animals whose bite may be very dangerous.

> STRANGER

Meaning?

DICK THORN

Meaning that I wish to compliment you for your colorful speech, but do not know how to repay you adequately for a most enlightening narrative.

STRANGER

Bah, it is nothing...

DICK THORN

You seemed to be speaking seriously.

STRANGER

And if that were so?

DICK THORN

Then you were trying to frighten me.

STRANGER

Not you, surely!

DICK THORN

Me, just like the others; I was there. I partook of the same emotions.

STRANGER

If you were there, you must have heard me reassuring my listeners by advising them to be incredulous.

DICK THORN

Then it was all a joke?

STRANGER

Of doubtful taste perhaps, but certainly quite innocent.

DICK THORN
Then perhaps you intended to mock me?

STRANGER
Mock you?

DICK THORN
Mock me—and the others. But let them take care of themselves. As for me—

STRANGER
As for you? You are greatly susceptible.

DICK THORN
Possibly, quite possibly, but I cannot allow someone to invent a diverting story so he can say: "I made Dick Thorn blanch."

STRANGER
Ah, indeed! It's a German quarrel you seek with me at the moment.

DICK THORN
I am Scottish, Sir, and our courage is proverbial. I can give you proof of that.
                    (unsheathing)
Attention, Virginia.

STRANGER
Oh! Oh! To unsheathe like that! To frighten the birds of this earthly paradise. To risk bloodying this happy fest…

DICK THORN

To bloody it, we would have to be certain that you have blood in your veins—for your ghostly pallor is that of a corpse.

STRANGER
(darkly)

My dear Captain, I fear you are going too far.

DICK THORN

Too far for you to follow me?

STRANGER

My pallor outrages you! Beware! If my cheeks are so pale that you can't see the rouge of the rage that flushes them, that's no reason to think that the blood which nevertheless rises to my face doesn't beat violently in my heart.

DICK THORN

It remains to be seen if it is from rage—or fear.

STRANGER
(unsheathing)

You wretch!

DICK THORN
(raising his blade)

Come on, Virginia, look at the stars.

STRANGER

You'll pay for your insolence!

They begin to cross swords.

DICK THORN

We'll see!

SIR WILLIAM
(aside)
He's succeeded.

The Stranger's blade pricks Dick Thorn.

STRANGER

Touché!

DICK THORN

My turn…Virginia, avenge yourself!

They fight furiously. Maxwell and Reginald return, followed by all the guests.

MAXWELL

What's going on?

REGINALD

A duel?

DICK THORN

An insolent foreigner whom I intend to punish.

TOM PLATT

O Lord!

MAXWELL AND REGINALD
Stop! Gentlemen! Stop!

But Dick Thorn runs the Stranger through; he falls with a scream.

DICK THORN
Too late! Virginia is avenged.

ALL
Oh!

TOM PLATT
My poor Master.

MAXWELL
(kneeling by the Stranger)
Perhaps I can still save him…

SIR WILLIAM
(to Dick Thorn)
What did he say?

DICK THORN
Don't worry. I know Virginia's thrust.

MAXWELL
His heart is still beating. Have him carried to my surgery.

DICK THORN
(looking at his sword)
Two inches in the liver. He'll die en-route. Doctor, you won't need any bandages.
(he resheathes his sword)

CURTAIN

Scene II

Maxwell's office. A door at the back gives on the garden. A door at the right. A large library filled with books, medical instruments, stuffed animals, viols, urns, glassware, skeletons and preserved heads. To the left, a canopied bed on a platform, protected by curtains running on rods. A lamp burns on the table.

AT RISE, Maxwell is alone, looking through the curtains toward the bed which is half open. A ray of light slips through the transept and strikes the face of the Stranger—Lord Ruthven—for it is he—stretched on the bed

MAXWELL

Dick Thorn's is a fine blade. The dressing was only placed on a cadaver. I swore I would bring him back to life, but I admit my impotence. I confess my shame.

(slowly moving away)

Now, here's all that a man can do! Destroy! Dick Thorn is king of the world! His blade is all powerful. It kills who it pleases. As for me, I have science. And I can do nothing against his power.

(returning to the foot of the bed)

Oh, everything's quite over. The wound is deep enough for the soul to be able to escape. He's dead! Quite dead! Heavens! Is that an illusion? Did I see his eye open? His hand move?

(he places his hand on the dead
man's chest)

Oh, no, no, not a heartbeat. He's dead, quite dead. And yet …

He runs to the library and pulls out an old book which he places on the table and thumbs through it feverishly.

MAXWELL

By all the Powers of Hell. Could it be?...
(reading)
"Don't deny vampires. The wisest minds have attested their existence. When the tomb shuts on them, they can emerge at night in the shape of ghosts."
(interrupting himself)
Ghosts! Visions born of fever or folly. This is naive.
(continues reading)
"The Vampire can be reborn three times. Life can return to the body when it is exposed to the action of lunar rays, before its remains have been confided to the Earth again; like a living man, it is subject to the chances other men run of death, and when for a third time, it has perished by a violent death, all resurrection is impossible. It returns to nothingness."
(rising)
I am confronting one of the most terrifying mysteries of Nature. What of the victims if I give in to the temptations of science? Won't the innocent pay for the guilty? Oh, that would be shocking! Remain dead, remain dead, cursed one. I won't be the one to revive you!

He violently closes the curtains of the canopy, then continues to read the book. Suddenly, there is a gentle knocking at the door.

MAXWELL

Someone's knocking?

The knocking becomes impatient.

MAXWELL

Who could it be?

After making certain the curtains are quite shut, he goes
to the door and opens it. It is Reginald.

REGINALD

It's me, Reginald!

MAXWELL

You, Reginald, at this hour?

REGINALD

Yes. Are you alone?

MAXWELL
(after casting a glance at the bed)
Alone, yes, I'm alone!

REGINALD
(turning towards the outside)
In that case, come in!

Anna enters dressed in a long mantle with a capuchin
domino.

MAXWELL

What does this mean?

ANNA
(removing the hood)
It's me, Maxwell!

Reginald shuts the door behind her.

MAXWELL

Anna! You here, at my place, at night!

ANNA

Yes. Tomorrow would have been too late.

MAXWELL

Why?

ANNA

I wanted to warn you, to beg you… I've come to tell you that I love you, but my father rules my destiny. He doesn't intend to give me to you. Please don't take arms against him…

MAXWELL

I hear you, and yet, I'm afraid of misunderstanding. The hope he let me glimpse…?

ANNA

You've got to renounce it.

MAXWELL

But just this evening…

ANNA

Earlier this evening, my father was merely Sir William Clifford, Baronet. But the title and fortune of the old Lord Ruthven will now come to him, and…

MAXWELL

He wasn't so confident yesterday.

REGINALD

He'd been told a legitimate heir existed.

MAXWELL

I see.

REGINALD

But now, Sir William is quite certain that this heir no longer lives and, in that case…

MAXWELL

In that case, there is an unbridgeable gap between us. I am poor because I've devoted my life to science, and my science to relieving the suffering of the poor. So it is madness for me to pretend to such an alliance.

REGINALD

My friend!

MAXWELL

Worse still, he will give Anna to someone else.

ANNA

No! Never!

MAXWELL

Oh, yes. He will command and you will have no choice but obey, and marry the one he's chosen for you.

ANNA

Maxwell, it seemed to me that my voice would soften the bitterness of his refusal. I was mistaken. If you lack courage, who will give me some?

MAXWELL

Anna! I am really suffering…

ANNA

Me, too!

MAXWELL

But you won't have either the will or the strength to fight back. And to know that, one day, I may see you in the arms of a rival…

ANNA

Maxwell…

MAXWELL

An odious rival!

REGINALD

Why would you have to see her like that?

MAXWELL

What do you mean?

REGINALD

What's forcing you to dwell is this country where life is so painful and sad for you?

MAXWELL

I…

REGINALD

No question Anna will marry someday. But you could choose to be unaware of it, if by a voluntary exile—

MAXWELL

Voluntary exile! Tell me that idea doesn't come from you. You're in love with my sister. You know she'd follow me anywhere.

REGINALD

Maxwell!

MAXWELL

I tell you, this idea didn't come from you. I smell the hand of proud Sir William... Insolent plebeian, I dared pretend to the hand of his daughter. So much audacity merits punishment. A refusal is not enough. He must drive me out!

REGINALD

Maxwell, you're becoming obsessed!

MAXWELL

Swear to me. Swear to me, both of you, that I'm wrong... Ah! You keep silent! So, I guessed right, didn't I?

ANNA

Yes, Maxwell, it is true. My father is cruel. He very much wishes you ill. He insists on your departure. I curse fate, but I cannot curse him, for he's my father, Maxwell—my father.

REGINALD

What's your decision, Maxwell?

MAXWELL

I don't know. Can I make a decision like this so fast? Can I tear my love from my heart? Is that what you came to ask of me, Anna?

ANNA

No!

MAXWELL

Good, for I would be unable to obey you.

ANNA

And yet, perhaps you should.

MAXWELL

To forget you? Oh, that's beyond your power. Don't ask the impossible of me.

ANNA

Whatever may happen, I have the right to tell you that I love you. I say it without blushing. Goodbye, Maxwell. I'm not telling you to leave, but the sight of you deprives me of the courage that I need. Spare me the spectacle of your suffering.

MAXWELL

I will obey you.

ANNA

Thank you. Goodbye. I love you. I will love you forever.

Maxwell kisses her hands. Anna gently disengages her-self.

REGINALD

Courage, Maxwell.

MAXWELL

Don't worry, I'll be brave.

Anna puts on her cloak, and offers her hand to Maxwell who kisses it. Maxwell shakes hands with Reginald. Then, they leave. Maxwell throws himself in an arm-chair.

MAXWELL

Why should I hesitate?

He pulls back the curtain and lets the moonlight bathe the body of Lord Ruthven.

MAXWELL

Ah, I am poor and obscure. Well, Sir William, I am going to prove to you that, from the depth of my poverty and obscurity, my vengeance can dazzle even someone as powerful as you. Come to life, mysterious creature, who can repay me with the blood of men. Fear not! I will be near you. And I won't allow you to revert to no-thingness, even after you've made the ones who've done so much ill to me expiate their crimes.

At this moment, the corpse moves its head and raises it.

MAXWELL

So the legends didn't lie…

MAXWELL (cont'd)

The soul seeks to resume its place. Life is flowing again in those icy veins. I am the equal of God, for I have created a new man. Bad luck—bad luck to the one who first falls beneath your glance.

Lord Ruthven rises on the bed and looks around confusedly. Suddenly, Fanny appears in the doorway.

FANNY

You're still awake?

Maxwell turns and sees his sister.

MAXWELL

Ah!

He rushes toward her to prevent her from entering.

MAXWELL

Get out of here!

FANNY
(surprised)
What's the matter with you?

MAXWELL
(fearful)
Get out of here! For God's sake, get out of here!

FANNY
(noticing Ruthven)
My God!

RUTHVEN
(noticing Fanny)
Ah, that young girl… How beautiful she is.

FANNY
That young man! You've saved him! Ah, your science is powerful, Maxwell.

MAXWELL
His glance on her. The Devil's work has begun. God is avenging himself already!

CURTAIN

ACT II

Scene III

A salon, tables, armchairs, etc.

AT RISE, Tom Platt is straightening the chairs around the table.

TOM PLATT
There. An armchair for the Sheriff. Another armchair for the heir. What an event!

Betsy emerges from an apartment.

BETSY
This is going to cause me a lot of trouble.

TOM PLATT
Heavens! Betsy, my fiancée.

BETSY
Yes, it's me. Mr. Tom.

TOM PLATT
And what brings you into the castle, Mrs. Platt?

BETSY
Mrs. Platt? Not yet!

TOM PLATT

But you will be—tomorrow.
(emphasizing)
Tomorrow, Miss Betsy—Why, it's tomorrow today.

BETSY

That's why I'm here.

TOM PLATT

Ah!

BETSY

You wouldn't have done it but for Miss Anna.

TOM PLATT

Yes, she promised to be present at our wedding.

BETSY

Miss Anna is not happy.

TOM PLATT

She's not like her father, then. Now there's one who
doesn't conceal his joy over the death of his cousin.
Why, his estate is now immense, more immense than
even those of that French Marquis—the Marquis de
Caubu.

BETSY

Has he ever been in Scotland? No one knows him here.

TOM PLATT

No, he's a pig in a poke.

BETSY

And is he rich?

TOM PLATT

He must be, since he's marrying Sir William's daughter. By the way, I heard that her father sent that man a wardrobe so that he could dress decently.

BETSY

What man?

TOM PLATT

Eh, by Jove, that big devil, that dung-bag. That miscreant, that ear-cutter…
(seeing Dick Thorn enter)
…That brave soldier! That noble sword! That valiant Captain Dick Thorn!

DICK THORN

(patting him on the shoulder)
Well said, my lad. Disinterested praise pleases me.

TOM PLATT

(bowing)
Captain.

DICK THORN

(going to Betsy)
Hey, who's this pretty little girl?

TOM PLATT

(placing himself between them and taking Betsy's arm)
My fiancée, Captain.

DICK THORN

Your fiancée… Such an Irish morsel. So you love this lucky dummy, my pretty-pretty?

BETSY

Hell, yes, Sir, Captain.

DICK THORN

Not possible.

TOM PLATT

Indeed so, actually. But your lordship no doubt wants to speak to my master. I'll go inform him.

DICK THORN

Go. Your charming fiancée will keep me company.

BETSY

With pleasure, Milord.

TOM PLATT
(placing himself between them again)
Didn't you just tell me that your aunt Sarah was expecting you at the tavern of Robert the Bruce?

BETSY

Why, no.

TOM PLATT

Yes. She must expect you. She'll be uneasy, poor woman. You must return right away. Night is coming on.

BETSY

It's not even noon.

TOM PLATT

Well, time's flying. Noon barely strikes and then its midnight. Come on!

BETSY

But…

TOM PLATT

Come on!
(low)
You flirt!
(aloud)
Your servant, Captain.
(low, quarreling with her)
A fine gallant to get involved with!

BETSY

Heavens, that's always fun!

She turns to curtsy to Dick Thorn. Tom Platt drags and pushes her.

DICK THORN
(twirling his mustache)
That poor lad is lucky. I don't have a single moment to steal from the serious business that brings me here. Because the sum agreed upon is truly not commensurate with the services rendered.

Noises off stage.

DICK THORN
Ah, it's Sir William... But he's not alone. Let's watch for a favorable opportunity.

He enters a room at the right and listens from the doorway.

The Sheriff enters with Sir William.

SHERIFF
I repeat, Sir William, I recognize your rights. The intention of the old Lord Ruthven, your relative, was not to leave his wealth without a legitimate heir indefinitely.

SIR WILLIAM
I think like you, my dear Sheriff.

SHERIFF
He looked on his daughter's son as his legitimate heir. But that son cannot inherit unless he is alive and present. So, if, in less than an hour, he does not appear, the law...

SIR WILLIAM
...Will recognize me as the legitimate heir to the title. But, if the grandson presents himself, I shall be ready to leave this castle without a murmur and return to my life of poverty...

SHERIFF
A most honorable course of action, if it is borne with courage and resignation. Till soon, my dear lord, till soon.

The Sheriff leaves.

SIR WILLIAM

Till soon, but not soon enough for my impatient whim.

Dick Thorn returns and taps him on the shoulder.

DICK THORN

A beautiful speech, Sir William!

SIR WILLIAM

What? Ah, it's you, Captain!

DICK THORN

A pity it had no other auditor than this good Sheriff.
(imitating Sir William)
But if the grandson presents himself… Joker! You know quite well that he'll never present himself—thanks to Dick Thorn and his infallible Virginia
(he raps the hilt of his sword)

SIR WILLIAM

Who received the agreed remuneration and must never again mention the subject.
(sitting down)

DICK THORN

(following him)
We've spelled out only the first page of our agreement.

SIR WILLIAM

(taken aback)
What? But it was you yourself who fixed the price!

DICK THORN

Bah! A total mistake! Virginia isn't very strong at arithmetic. And she didn't understand the importance of the succession.

SIR WILLIAM

And what is the succession worth in your opinion?

DICK THORN

The succession's worth a lot more, and I have a right to a modest share of it.

SIR WILLIAM

You do?

DICK THORN
(sitting next to Clifford)

We are far removed cousins in the 25th degree. Insufficient, perhaps, for the law to recognize my rights, but quite enough for the conscience of Sir William Clifford, newly minted Marquis of Ruthven, by the Grace of God, and Virginia's, to give me a little nibble of something.

SIR WILLIAM

Cousin near or far signifies nothing. What do you want?

DICK THORN

A little bonus, nothing more. Don't worry, I 'm not going to erect a genealogical tree to vindicate my rights, but when I tell myself that millions are at stake, I really find the purse you tossed me rather light and lean.

SIR WILLIAM

Look, state plainly what you are demanding.

He rises.

DICK THORN
Sit down, cousin, I haven't finished yet.

Sir William sits down.

DICK THORN
You are what you are only thanks to this devil of a captain and his incomparable Virginia. It's only just that you reward both in proportion to the service rendered. Your castle will be his, your table will be his, he will ride your best horses, and he will hunt foxes with your swiftest dogs.
(to Sir William who has risen again.)
Will you sit down, cousin, and let me finish.
(Sir William sits down again)
But perhaps it might be disagreeable to have a witness so close to remind one of one's obligations... So how to express gratitude, without having this annoying captain underfoot? I've got it! Give him the equivalent—a share of equal value to go and live in peace somewhere else in the country, and hang up Virginia, calm in her innocent scabbard.

SIR WILLIAM
(rising)
So how much are you demanding...?

DICK THORN
(rising in his turn)
Why, not much. You owe me everything, and that's got to be worth something.

SIR WILLIAM

If the Old Lord Ruthven's grandson was here, you would have nothing.

DICK THORN

True, true, and you no more than I. But do consider this: If I hadn't been here, that same grandson would be.

SIR WILLIAM

Until I am declared master here, I cannot say yes or no.

DICK THORN

Short of burying him yourself, you could hardly be more certain of his death.

SIR WILLIAM

Look here, I'll think about it, I'll consider...

DICK THORN

No, oh, no! Right away! It has to be done instantly.

SIR WILLIAM

Ah, these are unreasonable demands...

DICK THORN

Would you like to make Miss Anna our arbitrator?

SIR WILLIAM

My daughter? No, no. Let her remain unaware.

DICK THORN

Well, if you are so afraid of initiating her into our secret...

SIR WILLIAM
Well, surely...

DICK THORN
Think of her astonishment at seeing me established near you, and consequently near her. Decidedly, hesitation is not possible. Make me a gift of Blair Athol in County Perth. I know little about it, but I will take it on trust. It's agreed, right?

More noises off stage.

DICK THORN
I hear Miss Anna. I'll leave you with her. It's all agreed then; there's no reason to discuss it further. I'm going to get myself served a haunch of venison and a pint or two of ale. And when the Sheriff places you in possession of the title, you'll sign the act of gift to me. I'll be grateful all my life for that generosity, touched to the point of tears.

Anna enters.

DICK THORN
(to Anna)
Ah, Miss Anna, if you knew what kind of man your father is, you'd be astonished. Your father is truly the most generous of men!

Dick Thorn exits.

ANNA
What did he mean by that?

SIR WILLIAM

Nothing, nothing... He's a distant relative of ours, and I'm taking steps to assure his comfortable existence.

ANNA

You are so good, father, so generous...

SIR WILLIAM

Child...

ANNA

So why are you harsh with me alone?

SIR WILLIAM

Haven't I explained already?

ANNA

A ray of hope still penetrates my soul. Maxwell is full of talent, but he's poor, so our situation would be precarious, and my father worries over privations for me and that upsets him.

SIR WILLIAM

No question, that's indeed the motive for my decision.

ANNA

(excitedly)

But it's no longer important because, as of today, our fortune will...

SIR WILLIAM

...Erects an insurmountable barrier between you and the man you've chosen without the consent of your father.

SIR WILLIAM (cont'd)

I have confidence that, while he aspired to the hand of Anna Clifford, he wouldn't dare raise his eyes to the daughter of the Marquis of Ruthven.

ANNA

Then it would have been better for me to descend than to rise.

SIR WILLIAM

Your young girl's dreams will fade at the dazzle of your new situation. I am not going to sacrifice a brilliant future for you, to your naive dreams and the pretentions of a village doctor. So take that for decided, Anna, and never mention it to me again.

Sir William goes to the rear and looks outside.

ANNA

Ah, Betsy, Betsy! How I envy you.
                    (she collapses into a chair)

SIR WILLIAM

They're coming at last!

The Sheriff enters with Tom Platt and Dick Thorn.

SHERIFF

We're ahead of the hour by a few minutes, Milord.

SIR WILLIAM

Please do say "Sir William," Sheriff. Until the law has sanctioned my rights, I am only Baronet Clifford.

DICK THORN

My cousin William is splendid.

The Sheriff goes to the table prepared for him.

SHERIFF

It is time to proceed to the reading of the deceased Lord Ruthven's will before the two Assessors.

SIR WILLIAM

Where are they?

Maxwell and Reginald enter.

SHERIFF
(taking notice of then)

Here they are.

ANNA

Him!

SIR WILLIAM

Doctor Maxwell!

REGINALD

Don't be so surprised, Sir William. Accosted by the Sheriff, my friend and I were unable to recuse ourselves.

MAXWELL

A civic duty is a civic duty.

ANNA
(aside)

Has this last trial been reserved for me?

SHERIFF:
Please take your seats, Ladies and Gentlemen.

Everyone sits.

SHERIFF
Before placing Sir William in possession of the proper-
ties and titles of the late Marquis of Ruthven, I have to
give you information about his last wishes.

SIR WILLIAM
(aside, watching Maxwell)
Is it chance alone that brings this audacious pretender
here?

MAXWELL
(low to Reginald)
See how pale she is.

DICK THORN
(aside)
Pity I didn't have time to finish my steak.

SHERIFF
(reading)
"Ready to appear before God, I intend to make amends
for an injustice. I am dying alone and forsaken for having disregarded the laws of nature. Two spectres have
troubled my sleepless nights, that of my unforgiven dead
daughter, and that of her child, deprived of the fortune
that her name assured him. I'm unaware if he is living or
dead. Heaven, perhaps, won't leave me time to know. I
feel that my end is approaching…"

SHERIFF (cont'd)

"The information that I've sought has remained unanswered. Who knows if the disinherited son has not joined his cruelly abandoned mother in the tomb? If God does not permit me to rectify my sin, if I cannot annul a harsh sentence, if on the hour of the day fixed for opening the will, my grandson, the true Lord Ruthven, has not come to assume possession of my inheritance, then I shall take my punishment for such harsh inflexibility into eternity, and Sir William Clifford, my nearest relative, will become my sole heir."

The first stroke of noon strikes.

SIR WILLIAM
(aside, with barely controlled joy)
The hour, here's the hour.

SHERIFF
You've heard the will, Gentlemen. The hour's striking.
(in a loud voice)
I call the direct heir. I call Lord Ruthven. Some of you may know him...

DICK THORN
(aside)
Some of us did indeed.

SHERIFF
Can anyone here tell us where he is?

DICK THORN
(aside)
No fear that I will speak.

Meanwhile, the clock continues to strike.

SHERIFF
(low to Sir William)
Vain action, but it's customary by law.

SIR WILLIAM
Do it!

SHERIFF
In the name of the law, we summon whoever has rights to the estate of the deceased Lord Ruthven to present himself on this very hour if he does not wish to be deprived of his rights forevermore.

MAXWELL
The abyss is deepening profoundly.

SHERIFF
For the last time, we demand—

Tom Platt enters.

TOM PLATT
(announcing)
Lord Ruthven!

General reaction.

ALL
Him?

DICK THORN
What?
(to Sir William)
In that case, who did you have me kill?

ANNA
Maxwell. My hope is reborn!

On the 12th stroke, Lord Ruthven, the "Stranger," appears.

RUTHVEN
I am precise to the hour, sir.

CLIFFORD, DICK THORN, MAXWELL
(each with his own unique reaction)
Him!

SHERIFF
Sir, are you furnished with all the proper evidence?

RUTHVEN
Indeed I am. Here are my documents; they prove beyond dispute that I am the son of Lucy Ruthven and George Stritza, and that I have the right to take the title and the name of my late grandfather.
(he sits down)

SHERIFF
(after looking)
The documents are in order.

SIR WILLIAM
But…

RUTHVEN

Oh, I understand your surprise—(emphasizing)Baronet.
Doubtless, you've heard of a certain quarrel, a duel, that
was to be funereal for me. Certainly, I ought to be lying
in a grave at this hour, but I owe it to the most adroit of
doctors, past or future. He closed my wound; he revived
the last breath of a life ready to depart. I don't know how
to appreciate this service, but I shall maintain an eternal
gratitude to my miracle doctor—Edward Maxwell.

ALL

Maxwell!

SIR WILLIAM
(aside, furious)
Ah, it's to him that I owe—

RUTHVEN
(to Reginald)
You will not refuse to certify, sir?

REGINALD

What must I certify, sir?

RUTHVEN

That I was at that fest, and, despite the furious assault of
this valiant Captain…
(pointing to Dick Thorn)
I am still alive, thank God, though desolated to destroy
the hopes of Sir William, but quite ready to offer him
consolation.

SIR WILLIAM
(haughtily)

Milord, I completely accept things from the Hand of Fate, not from those of men. In your default, I would have become the possessor of these estates. You alive, I give thanks to God, and I remain in the modest condition in which, for the last fifty years, I have lived, respected by all. Goodbye, Milord

Taking Anna by the hand, Sir William starts to leave,

RUTHVEN
(noticing Anna, rising)

Heavens, stay, sir. You are proud, Sir William, and are scornful of my words. God preserve me from offending your honorable poverty. But aren't you terrified for your daughter?

SIR WILLIAM

My daughter—my sweet Anna?

RUTHVEN

Her hand is not promised to anyone?

SIR WILLIAM

To no one.

RUTHVEN

Well, don't you see in that a means of repairing the injustice of Fate? The pride of a relative may be affronted by an offer he considers as alms, but a father can, without shame, accept all from a prospective son-in-law.

SIR WILLIAM

A prospective son-in-law…

RUTHVEN

Much can be yours if you place Anna's hand in mine.

ALL

Miss Anna!

DICK THORN

Heavens! He's right.

ANNA

Father! Please!

SIR WILLIAM
(making up his mind)

Greet your cousin, Anna. As of tomorrow you'll be his wife—Lady Ruthven.

MAXWELL
(exploding)

His wife! Heaven and Earth! That's impossible!

ANNA, REGINALD

Maxwell!

RUTHVEN
(coldly)

I do not understand!

SIR WILLIAM

Pardon him, Milord. He's a rival...

RUTHVEN

(to Maxwell)

A rival! Ah, I understand and I excuse you. Poor Doctor Maxwell, you love Miss Anna. I can conceive that. I owe you everything, Doctor, but to tear the love I feel for her from me would be to tear away my life. You cannot ravish me of what you've so miraculously given me.

MAXWELL

You owe me your life? You! No, my science was only vanity. A miracle happened, yes, but it was a miracle from Hell.

ALL

From Hell?

MAXWELL

Sir William, banish all suspicion from your heart. Yes, I love your daughter, but it's not a jealous lover speaking to you. The man who is asking for your daughter, I saw him dead, his heart had ceased to beat. On my honor, on my Christian faith, I swear it to you.

RUTHVEN

No one disputes that I had already one foot in the grave, but you pulled it out.

MAXWELL

No, no! Not me, but a supernatural, mysterious, terrifying power.

RUTHVEN

My God! What a crazy idea! Sorrow has completely robbed you of your sanity.

SHERIFF
Madness indeed!

RUTHVEN
How else to explain this bizarre talk?

MAXWELL
Madness! Yes, madness troubles my thought when I think that she will become the victim of this monster. Because she's mine.

TOM PLATT
Now it's him, poor doctor!

MAXWELL
My God! Punishment wasn't slow coming. Please God! I implore you, let your anger fall on me, but spare the innocent victims of my impiety.

RUTHVEN
You hear him! Was I wrong to call him mad?

SIR WILLIAM
Tomorrow, Lord Ruthven, the chaplain of your ancestor's castle will bless your marriage to my daughter.

RUTHVEN
Thank you, father.

ANNA
(collapsing onto a chair)
Lost! I am lost!

MAXWELL

Tomorrow! Tomorrow! Oh, no! Before tomorrow, monster thirsty for blood, you'll return to the tomb!

SHERIFF

This is too much to put up with any longer.

RUTHVEN

My friends, this unfortunate that reason has abandoned has the right to all our cares.

DICK THORN

He's completely mad!

MAXWELL

Mad! Ah, I shall be! I am already. My head is on fire. Anna! Anna! Midnight strikes. The dead emerge from their graves. Have no fear! All my blood if need be will be spent to repurchase yours.

He falls exhausted. Reginald supports him. The Sheriff gestures to his men to approach him. Lord Ruthven approaches Anna to reassure her. She rises and recoils in terror. Sir William reacts angrily, but is restrained by the ever-calm Ruthven.

CURTAIN

ACT III

Scene IV

An inn in the Scottish mountains, some miles from Edinburgh. There are shrubs, trees—it is a picturesque sight. At the rear, right and left, are hills leading to the mountain. To the right, the entrance to the inn. To the left, a pavilion with a door, window and usable balcony. Clumps of trees, tables, chairs.

AT RISE, Fanny and her Aunt Sarah, both dressed in traveling attire, have just arrived at the inn in a carriage. Their presence has been noticed by Betsy, who is preparing for her wedding. Also present is Hurley, a local servant.

BETSY
(to Hurley)
Hurley, take Miss Fanny's horses in the stable. Give them a good feed and also provide lunch for the driver.

Hurley leaves to the right.

FANNY
My dear Betsy, I assure you, it's impossible for us to stay here. We must continue on our route.

BETSY
Come on! You'd have the heart to pass by our inn without stopping, and on the day I'm getting married?

FANNY

My brother insists that I leave Edinburgh. Why? I don't know, but I must obey him.

BETSY

But you're quite a distance from Edinburgh. That's the main thing. I'm not going to let you leave. I'm getting married and I've got no one from our town at my wedding. Miss Anna cannot come. Stay for the party, the dancing, and tomorrow morning, continue your trip.

FANNY

But if Maxwell knew I was disobeying him, I'd incur his wrath, and I don't want to do that.

BETSY

Well, we won't tell him. I'll take it all on myself.
(to Fanny's Aunt Sarah who's remained
standing, twisting and twiddling her thumbs)
C'mon, Aunt Sarah, no more twiddling your thumbs like a mill wheel. Help me convince our dear Fanny.

AUNT SARAH

Duty calls! I obey!

BETSY

Fanny! How could you stop by this inn without even saying hello—that's bad, very bad. Luckily, I had my nose out the window as you were sneaking by.

AUNT SARAH
(to Fanny)
My dear child! Listen to her!

FANNY

But if my brother knew…

BETSY

Who's going to tell him? Not I, certainly. Look, Aunt Sarah agrees with me. The guests are dancing, drinking ale... You like ale...

AUNT SARAH

Myself, I love it.

BETSY

They're eating ham.

AUNT SARAH

Ham!

BETSY

And whiskey too. There'll be plenty of whiskey!

AUNT SARAH

Whiskey!

BETSY

And the jig. We'll dance the jig later! You're my oldest friend. You cannot not stay for the wedding.

AUNT SARAH
(dancing)

The jig.

BETSY

It'll be a lot of fun. Tell me you'll stay, right?

SARAH

(to Fanny)

Betsy's right, Miss Fanny. Who would tell your brother that we've stopped en route? Today, we should enjoy the feast. We'll laugh, we'll dance the jig... Drink some whiskey... Eat some ham... and tomorrow morning, we'll resume our journey.

FANNY

My good Aunt Sarah!

AUNT SARAH

You're my niece, after all.

FANNY

Oh, well, OK then... If there are reproaches later, I'll accept them.

Betsy makes Fanny sit.

TOM PLATT

(off stage)

Betsy! Betsy!

BETSY

Ah, my fiancé.

Tom Platt enters.

TOM PLATT

Betsy! Betsy!

(seeing Fanny and Aunt Sarah)

Ah, Miss Fanny, Aunt Sarah—at our wedding. What an honor!

BETSY

Miss Fanny will continue the trip she's been ordered to take tomorrow morning.

TOM PLATT

Excellent! Oh, Aunt Sarah, let me kiss you. I've shaved.
                    (kisses her, then Betty)
Hum! Hum!

BETSY
                    (amused)
Will you mind!

Tom pays no attention to her and kisses Fanny. Then, he points to the pavilion at left.

TOM PLATT

The ladies will sleep in the room next to ours. It's got white curtains.
                    (making Aunt Sarah dance)
We'll dance a jig
                    (to Fanny)
The curtains are quite new.
                    (to Aunt Sarah)
And we'll drink! Put the horses in the stable!

BETSY

Why, that's been done already, you blockhead!

TOM PLATT

Oh, Aunt Sarah! Betsy will make me lose my mind!
                    (making her dance)
We'll jig together, First, though—Hurley! Hurley!

AUNT SARAH

What a crazy man!

TOM PLATT

With you, yes.

Hurley returns.

HURLEY

You called, Master Tom?

TOM PLATT

Yes. Straighten up the large room in the pavilion.
(to Betsy)
Ah, Betsy, for me this day is full of stars!

FANNY

(to Sarah)
Since we are staying, I am giving you complete freedom for the day.

SARAH

Oh, Miss Fanny, are you? You are too kind!

TOM PLATT

Yes, yes. And me, too. I'm nice. I love Betsy!
(hugging Betsy, then low to Hurley)
Understood, right? The inn is closed for today. No bargaining. Let them go elsewhere.

BETSY

What? Not at all! If travelers come, let them be received. They can celebrate with us. It's a party for everybody!

BETSY (cont'd)

For payment, they need only wish us well in our marriage.

TOM PLATT

Well said. I wasn't thinking of that!

We hear shooting outside.

TOM PLATT

Ah, now there's the wedding party. They're coming to
take us to church.

BETSY

I'm going to finish dressing.

TOM PLATT

That's the thing; Make yourself beautiful
(kissing her)
Beautiful! Beautiful!

BETSY

Will you quit!

Betsy leaves to get dressed. A group of peasants enter,
followed by the rest of the wedding party.

TOM PLATT

(to the peasants)
Over this way, over this way, the rest of you.
(to the others)
Stop the music. Form up over there!

FIRST PEASANT

Don't worry, lad. The muskets are loaded. It's gonna be
magnificent

TOM PLATT

That's the thing. Hurley! Hurley!

Hurley comes to Tom.

TOM PLATT

Ale by the boatload!

Hurley leaves.

TOM PLATT

Let 'em swim and dance in ale!

Servants bring in pots of ale and cups.

PEASANT

Why you're going to drown your wedding!

TOM PLATT

Don't be afraid, I'll fish 'em out.
                    (making a swimming gesture)
You know how to swim?

Drinks are poured.

FANNY
            (sad)
My poor brother.

Aunt Sarah takes a cup and offers it to Tom.

AUNT SARAH
A cup for me. Just a drop, for it's soon done.

TOM PLATT
(pouring)
Never too soon! Drink up, Aunt Sarah! There are twenty more casks in the cellar.
(to Fanny)
Miss Fanny, have a cup of ale, to do like everybody else!

FANNY
(taking the cup and drinking)
To the health of the married couple!

TOM PLATT
Thank you, Miss Fanny! Thank you, my friends!

Fanny sits back down.

AUNT SARAH
(extending her cup)
Another cup, just for a taste.

TOM PLATT
Always happy to oblige!

He pours her another drink. Just then, Allison, a maid, enters.

ALLISON
(announcing)
Ladies and gentlemen—the bride is ready!

TOM PLATT

Attention, the rest of you! Miss Fanny, my apologies, we're going to make some smoke.

FANNY

Don't worry about me.

ALLISON

Here comes the bride!

ALL

Long live the wedding couple!

They discharge their muskets. Betsy enters, dressed in a beautiful white gown.

BETSY

Thank you! Thank you!

TOM PLATT

Let's get on our way to church
            (to Fanny)
Miss Fanny, would you allow me?
            (offering her his arm)

FANNY

My good Tom, Betsy, will you excuse me from going to church? I need freshen up after our long journey.

TOM PLATT

As you will, Miss Fanny.

BETSY

We're going to show you your room.
(to Allison)
Allison, please escort Miss Maxwell.

ALLISON

Certainly.

TOM PLATT

Ah, Hurley! Am I dumb to forget this! The best room is
reserved for Lord Ruthven.

FANNY
(excitedly)
Lord Ruthven!

TOM PLATT

Yeah! Our good lord deigns to be present at our feast.
He's probably already waiting for us at the church.

ALL

Ah!

TOM PLATT

What an honor, huh?

FANNY

That man, here…

TOM PLATT
(to the peasants)
Don't be afraid, the rest of you. He's a bit pale, but a
good master. Come on! Musicians in the lead. The rest
follow. Goodbye. Miss Fanny.

BETSY

Thank you, Miss Fanny! Till soon

They file out in front of Fanny.

FANNY
(aside)
I'm scared. But why? It's ridiculous to be frightened of
Lord Ruthven. A skinny little man like that…
(going toward the back)
My God! Maxwell and Reginald here. If he sees me,
what will he say?
(to Allison)
Quick, take me the room they've given me!

ALLISON

In this pavilion, Miss.

FANNY

Lead me, lead me!

ALLISON

Come!

They leave. Maxwell enters, followed by Reginald.

MAXWELL

We've arrived.

REGINALD

At last! Since we left Edinburgh, I've hardly been able
to get you to unclench your teeth. Now that we're here,
perhaps you'll relax and explain the purpose of this mysterious voyage?

MAXWELL

Soon, Reginald, soon…

Alison returns, alone.

MAXWELL
(to Allison)
One word, young lady.

ALLISON

Two, if you'd like.

MAXWELL

Is this Wakefield?

ALLISON

Yes.

MAXWELL

Miss Betsy's inn?

ALLISON

Yes. At the moment, she's marrying Tom Platt, a valet of the new Lord Ruthven.

MAXWELL

Is His Lordship here?

ALLISON

We're all expecting him, sir. It's a great honor for the newlyweds.

MAXWELL

Thank you, Miss. Now would you serve us a pot of ale?

ALLISON

Right away!

FANNY
(spying them from the balcony)
Both of them here... What have they come here to do?

REGINALD
(to Maxwell)
Why all these questions? All these mysteries?

ALLISON
(with a pot of ale and cups)
Here, gentlemen!

MAXWELL
(sitting down)
Thank you, Miss!

Allison leaves, looking askance at Maxwell.

MAXWELL

Drink, Reginald, drink. Make yourself giddy if you can.
(pressing Reginald's hand)
Reginald, look me carefully in the face...

REGINALD

I am looking at you, Maxwell.

MAXWELL

Since yesterday, I've gotten paler, right?

REGINALD

Yes, it's true—and to speak frankly, at this very moment, you scare me.

MAXWELL

Meaning that doubts have given way to certainty.

REGINALD

Maxwell…

MAXWELL

Don't deny it! You defended me yesterday when they said I was mad. But today, you're not so sure…

REGINALD

Maxwell…

MAXWELL

I'm tempted to believe I'm mad myself, but it wasn't folly that compelled me—it was remorse.

REGINALD

Remorse?

FANNY
(in her balcony)

Remorse?

MAXWELL

Yes, Reginald. My science is cursed. I meddled with impenetrable mysteries. My impious eye has sounded the depths of the tomb, and from there, I have made an infernal monster appear.

REGINALD

What are you saying?

Fanny stretches to listen.

MAXWELL

Three days ago, you laughed at the notion of those creatures whose lives continue after death, but they exist, those vampires live!

REGINALD

You are delirious, my friend!

MAXWELL

No, once again, it's not delirium. I tell you, I snatched one of these mysterious beings from the tomb. Death had frozen his body, stiffened his limbs, stopped the beating of his heart…

REGINALD

Folly!

MAXWELL

Truth!

REGINALD

The dreams of a troubled mind!

MAXWELL

Truth, I tell you, truth! When I ought to have thrust the monster into his terrible nothingness, I myself directed towards him the rays that recalled him to life. The Vampire is—Ruthven!

REGINALD

Ruthven!

FANNY

Oh!

MAXWELL

And do you imagine that God has been slow to avenge
Himself? Sir William thrust Anna into the arms of this
execrable monster. He's sending his daughter to her
death, because that demon needs the blood of a virgin to
survive.

REGINALD

This is horrible!

FANNY

Yes, yes, quite horrible.

MAXWELL

More horrible even than you think! Fanny, too, is an appointed sacrifice. That's why I sent her away.

REGINALD

Oh, that shall not be!

MAXWELL

It shall be. Hell wishes it so.

REGINALD

No! God will permit you to destroy your cursed work.
You made Ruthven emerge from the tomb; you must
make him go back!

MAXWELL

No, Reginald. My sword would break, bullets would bounce back from his breast. Even poison would be impotent.

REGINALD

Well, as for me, I will attempt it.

MAXWELL

You strike him. And when the tomb shuts on him, I will prevent him from emerging.

Fanny withdraws from the balcony.

REGINALD

Now I understand why you wanted to come here.

MAXWELL

Yes! He won't fail to cast himself on the prey for which he lusts.

REGINALD

Yet another?

MAXWELL

Yes. Betsy.

REGINALD

The poor girl.

MAXWELL

Indeed.

REGINALD

My courage is not shaken. I will try to warn Betsy of the peril that threatens her. And if my advice is disregarded, I will kill Ruthven.

MAXWELL

Do so! And I will nail him inside his tomb. If he's close to her... If he imagines she's in his power...

REGINALD

We're not there yet! Come on! To appear before him, you must compose your face. Otherwise your emotion will warn him something's afoot.

The two of them leave. Fanny reenters from the pavilion.

FANNY

I'm glad I learned this terrifying revelation. I will ward off the danger that threatens Anna. No more traveling.
(wrapping herself in her cloak)
I'll leave. It's to the castle of Ruthven that my destiny calls me. I must be there before the evening, even if I get there with bloodied feet. My God, please sustain me.

She leaves. The newlyweds enter with the marriage party, including Lord Ruthven, carrying cups and pots of ale.

ALL

Long live the newlyweds!

TOM PLATT

And long live, Milord Ruthven!

ALL

Long live Milord Ruthven!

RUTHVEN

Thank you, my friends, thank you.
(to Betsy)
My dear Betsy, I envy your husband's happiness.

BETSY

Thank you, Milord!

Ruthven takes Betsy's hand in his.

RUTHVEN

How happy he must be—because you are simply so beautiful.

BETSY
(aside)
This is singular. He frightens me, yet his voice charms me.

RUTHVEN

Don't take your hand away. Let me tell you all the sweet emotions that the sight of you engenders in my soul.

BETSY

Oh, Milord!

TOM PLATT

Come on, the rest of you! Let's laugh, sing. and drink again. Let's keep drinking!

Reginald and Maxwell enter.

REGINALD
I, too, ask to empty a glass to Betsy's health!

TOM PLATT
Ah, Mr. Reginald! Doctor Maxwell!

RUTHVEN
(aside)
Him!

TOM PLATT
You're right in time. The whole town's coming. Be welcome, Doctor! Let's drink to the health of the doctor who watches over us!

REGINALD
(to Ruthven)
Charmed, Milord, to meet you here.

MAXWELL
Quite a lucky chance!

RUTHVEN:
(aside)
Is he pursuing me?

BETSY
(aside)
Lord Ruthven's glance makes me tremble.

TOM PLATT
Come on, friends! To the health of Doctor Maxwell!

Everyone drinks, as do Reginald and Maxwell.

RUTHVEN

Don't lower your beautiful eyes, Betsy, and tell me if you're happy about my presence here.

BETSY

Oh, how can you ask me that?

MAXWELL
(to Reginald)

Look!

REGINALD

I see. The vulture's fascinating the pigeon. Wait.
(aloud)
The wedding's not complete. We drink, we laugh, but we must also sing. Come on, all!

ALL

That's the thing, that's the thing.

REGINALD

Pour once more and I'll begin

Drinks are poured to all the guests.

REGINALD
(singing)
From the breast of shadowy thickets
Where all sleep
Sometimes funereal shouts emerge
A sign of death.

Slowly flying from tree to tree
A black crow screeches.
The monster raises the marble
Of his tomb;
It's the smell of blood
That attracts him.
Beware! Young girl with vermilion blood
He's here, he's there!
Lying in wait,
For you to sleep.
It's the vampire!

ALL

Oh!

RUTHVEN
(aside)

Cursed song!

TOM PLATT

That's pretty sad. But the second half is amusing.

REGINALD (still singing)

The lord of haughty mien
With his pale face
Was sleeping beneath the stone yesterday
Laid out.
When at the ghosts' midnight hour
Echoed
Through the depths of the dark kingdom
He emerged
It's the smell of blood
That attracts him.

REGINALD (singing, cont'd)
Beware! Young girl with vermilion blood, etc.

BETSY
(aside)
Is it a warning?

RUTHVEN
(aside)
Won't this man ever finish?

TOM PLATT
Oh, that will make you shiver. I laughed like a madman.
Third Stanza, Mr. Reginald, please!

REGINALD (singing)
Does the mouth of the spectre
Dare speak of love?
Ply a rebellious ear
Wait for morning.
When the horizon darkens again
Burning purple
The damned driven out by dawn
Will disappear.
It's the smell of blood
That attracts him.
Beware! Young girl with vermilion blood, etc.

RUTHVEN
Oh, enough, sir. You are terrifying these good folk!

BETSY
Yes, yes, it makes me cold!

REGINALD
(to Maxwell)
The victim will be on her guard.

RUTHVEN
(aside)
He's shocked the girl

TOM PLATT
I got goose flesh from it. Come, come, let's think of eating and drinking. Vampires may be fun but they're not filling. Let's see if the table is set.

ALL
That's the thing, that's the thing.

RUTHVEN
(to Betsy)
Stay Betsy, I would like to speak to you.

BETSY
But…

RUTHVEN
(hypnotic)
Stay/

REGINALD
(to Maxwell)
Plant jealousy in the mind of the husband and Betsy's saved. Come!

They leave by the right.

RUTHVEN

Betsy, my sweet Betsy, harken to me!

BETSY

I ought not to *harken* to anything. A secret voice tells me
I will lose my happiness if I *hark* to your words.

RUTHVEN

On the contrary, your happiness will commence. Don't
you understand that I love you!

BETSY

Me!

RUTHVEN

Yes, you! Do you really want to be the wife of a servant? You know very well that you were made for better
things. Your heart is throbbing as it listens to me. I love
you, Betsy, I love you!

BETSY

You're scaring me!

RUTHVEN

I love you. I am rich, powerful... These riches could be
yours, my power could be yours.

BETSY

I tell you, You're scaring me!

RUTHVEN

Raise your eyes to mine. I insist on it—you must!. Let
the fire in my eyes intoxicate you; let your soul be filled
with my soul, let your heart beat against mine...

RUTHVEN (cont'd)

Only one kiss. Give it to me, Betsy. I love you, I love you, I love you!

BETSY

Ah, I feel I'm dying!

RUTHVEN

Tonight, soon, in an instant, we'll flee together, and you'll be mine, all mine!

BETSY

Help!

RUTHVEN
(taking her in his arms)

Silence! You are my life! My life, do you hear? And I won't give it to the one who made you his wife. Betsy, I tell you once again, I love you. You are mine!
(kissing her)

Tom Platt reenters and sees them.

TOM PLATT
(aside)

It's just as Mr. Reginald told me.
(To Ruthven)

Excuse me, Milord, I know you don't want to be bothered… And you're my master, of course… But may I ask what you were doing?

RUTHVEN
(bold)

I was kissing your wife, Tom

TOM PLATT

I can see that well enough.

RUTHVEN

To congratulate her on her happiness.

TOM PLATT

I'll be responsible for that all by myself, thank you, Milord, all by myself indeed.
                    (to Betsy)
You little flirt!

BETSY

Are you jealous?

TOM PLATT

I dunno. I hate to see him hold you like that. But I'm his
servant. Still, It's up to me to do his work, it's not for
him to do mine.
                    (aside)
You bet I'm jealous, and I'm going to keep my eye out.

BETSY
                (aside, looking at Ruthven)
In spite of myself, my eyes keep seeking out his.'

The guests return.

ALLISON

Well, Mr. Tom what about the dance?

ALL

Yes, yes, the dance! The dance!

TOM PLATT

Yes! The dance! Night's coming. Let lights be brought, and let's start the dance.
(to Betsy)
You shan't dance with anyone else, except me.

They light the room with torches.

BETSY
(eyes still on Ruthven who fascinates her)
But…

TOM PLATT

With me, I said! Let's dance a jig. Strike up the band!

The dance begins. Lord Ruthven eyes Betsy and fascinates her even as they dance.

BALLET

RUTHVEN
(near Betsy)
I love you, I love you.

His glance plunges into her. Outside, we hear Reginald's voice singing the refrain of his song. Everyone turns toward the sound of his voice.

REGINALD (outside, singing)
It's the smell of blood that attracts him
Beware! Young girl with vermilion blood
He's here, he's there!
Lying in wait,

REGINALD (singing, cont'd)

For you to sleep.
It's the vampire!

BETSY

My God! I'm scared! I'm so scared!

She leaves quickly and goes into the pavilion. Discreetly, Ruthven follows her.

TOM PLATT
(listening)
Oh, it's Mr. Reginald.
(turning)
Let's continue.
(not seeing Betsy, he mistakes
her disappearance)
Betsy! Where are you? Betsy! Where's wife! Well, well,
ah, the witch! Which way did they go?

He runs out to the right.

ALL

What's wrong with him. Is he mad?

BETSY
(outside)
Help! Help me! Please, help!

ALL

What are those screams?

Maxwell enters, followed by Reginald.

MAXWELL

Quick! He's strangling his victim!

He strides into the pavilion.

BETSY

Help! Help!

ALL

Let's go help her!

Tom returns.

TOM: PLATT

Where are they ? Where are they?

A shot is heard. He falls and screams.

ALL

Ah!

Everyone runs away, terrified.

TOM PLATT

I am dead!

MAXWELL

My God. Are my tortures over?
                    (seeing Reginald)
What happened to Betsy?

A very weak Betsy appears, supported by Allison. They
are followed by Aunt Sarah, pale and disheveled.

REGINALD
There's no longer anything to fear.

AUNT SARAH:
She's safe... But Miss Fanny...

MAXWELL AND REGINALD
(noticing her)
Aunt Sarah? What about Miss Fanny?

MAXWELL
My sister was here? What's happened to her? Where is she?

AUNT SARAH
I don't know. She's gone, gone... I don't know where...

REGINALD
Gone! But why? What were you doing here?

AUNT SARAH
(trembling)
Oh! I'm afraid. I don't know! I don't know!

REGINALD
Where did she go?

AUNT SARAH
I don't know! I don't know!

REGINALD:
(hurling himself on her)
Speak, you wretched woman!

MAXWELL
My sister! Oh, this is infernal.

REGINALD
She's not running any further danger. Our enemy is dead. We will find her. Come! Come!

They rush out. At this moment, the Moon comes to light the hill at the back. Hardly have they gone when Lord Ruthven, injured, dying, appears on the balcony.

RUTHVEN
Wounded. I am mortally wounded.

BETSY
(looking up and seeing him)
Ah! It's him! It's him!

She tugs Sarah and Allison back, shocked.

RUTHVEN
(alone on the balcony)
And by him, by that cursed Doctor... But I must still live... Ah, that ray of moonlight. It's life itself to me... But how to get to it.... Ah, the balcony.... Powers of Hell, give me the strength....

He grabs the balcony, climbs over it, and slides with a thousand sufferings and, at last, falls to the ground.

RUTHVEN
(dragging himself)
All my strength is going with my blood...

RUTHVEN (cont'd)

If only I could reach that hill, and place my face under the luminous ray of the Moon... But I can't, I'm choking... Shadows surround me. My eyes are veiled. Oh, light, light, will you come to reach me... Come to me... Pass over my face, even if only for one minute! Ah! No, no... I cannot do it...

He rises, then falls back.

CURTAIN

ACT IV

Scene V

A cemetery. Moonlight. In the midst of half-broken-down tombs, there's a new one, more visible than the others, on which are these words: LORD RUTHVEN.

AT RISE, Maxwell enters slow, terrified, holding a stake in his hand.

MAXWELL
Finally, I'm here. Despite myself, I'm shivering.

Recoiling, he touches Ruthven's tomb, then draws back in shock.

MAXWELL
Let's summon up the strength necessary.

He walks around the tomb and finally ends up back where he started.

MAXWELL
(reading)
"Lord Ruthven," "Lord Ruthven…" I will make sure you do not emerge from that tom again…

Midnight strikes lugubriously in the distance.

MAXWELL

Nothingness. Become nothing once more.

He takes up his stake, when a ghost rises up before him.

MAXWELL

Ah, who goes there? A spectre! Ah, ah! Is it your ghost who's come to thwart me, vampire? Well, my mind won't allow itself to be disturbed by these apparitions. Ghosts don't exist!

At this moment, he finds himself facing a second ghost, and the moonlight falls on Ruthven's tomb

MAXWELL

Another one?

A third ghost rises up.

MAXWELL

And another? Ah, ah! Spectres, Ghosts! You don't scare me! Get back! Get back! You won't prevent me from reaching the tomb to destroy my criminal work.

He rushes toward the tomb; the stone rises under a ray of moonlight. The last stroke of midnight rings.

MAXWELL

Ah! It's him! It's him!

Lord Ruthven rises. His shroud falls off; he appears fully clothed as in the preceding act.

MAXWELL

I'm too late! Too late!

Lord Ruthven bursts into strident laughter.

CURTAIN

Scene VI

Same salon as in Act III. AT RISE, Sir William is seated while Dick Thorn paces around uneasily.

SIR WILLIAM
(worried)
You've cut a slice of this very thick York Ham, you've feast on it with appetite, and then you've washed it down with several pints of ale.

DICK THORN
Meaning, that I am in no condition to express my ideas?

SIR WILLIAM
No, but those ideas are garbled. Bodily malaise prevents good mental work.

DICK THORN
My ideas are clear enough for all that. If you follow my advice, you will live out the rest of your days at peace with your conscience.

SIR WILLIAM
My conscience be damned! No, by all the Saints of Scotland, it shall not be! I refuse to follow the advice of stupid terror. I prefer the path that leads to fortune.

DICK THORN
And leads your daughter to despair or death.

SIR WILLIAM
(mockingly)
I am grateful for such touching solicitude, but I can only accept reasonable advice that is in my own interest.

DICK THORN
But what about mine ? God damn me, to let these things go, to see this marriage consummated... Why am I speaking against my own interest? Because, at bottom, there remains the residue of an honest man in me, that I don't want to allow to grow moldy. You daughter's tears...

SIR WILLIAM
Her tears have already dried.

DICK THORN
And Maxwell's revelation.

SIR WILLIAM
The delusions of a dismissed rival and a sick mind.

DICK THORN
Well my mind is even sicker then, because I've talked to Maxwell—twice, too!

SIR WILLIAM
(rising)
What? Ah, Dick, tell me you're not speaking seriously?

DICK THORN
Indeed, I am, quite seriously.

SIR WILLIAM
Do you remember what he said?

DICK THORN
I can repeat it word for word.

SIR WILLIAM
He claims to have held Lord Ruthven dead in his arms.

DICK THORN
Completely dead.

SIR WILLIAM
Who was it then who presented? An impostor?

DICK THORN
No, not at all.

SIR WILLIAM
A vampire then?

DICK THORN
Nothing else.

SIR WILLIAM
So you believe in vampires after all?

DICK THORN
I believe that those who have had the perilous honor of
being skewered by Virginia do not return in the flesh.

SIR WILLIAM
Are you intending to send me back to childhood, Dick?
Let's abandon the old wives' nursery tales and be men.

DICK THORN
But, by Saint Duncan, it can't have been a man that I had on the point of my sword—an ordinary man couldn't have returned from the grave!

SIR WILLIAM
Dick, you have a very naive confidence in the infallibility of your sword. Maybe your hand shook, or your sword went astray... The result was that you left the inheritance fall in other hands than mine. Your work has miscarried; mine has only begun, and all the sensitivities of a swordsman who's turning senile won't prevent me from seizing the compensations that fortune offers me. I shall remain Sir William Clifford, Baronet, but my daughter will be Lady Ruthven.

DICK THORN
Perhaps I am in the wrong and this Maxwell has made me share his madness. Perhaps I did miss killing my adversary as you said, but...
>   (picturing the thrust he gave)
...One, two, I felt Virginia slip between his ribs. He was dead. He had to be dead.
>   (with conviction to Clifford)
You'll be the father-in-law of a dead man.

Anna enters.

DICK THORN
>   (aside)
Poor girl! Please Heaven she may have heard me.

He moves away.

ANNA

(pensive)

Why am I so agitated? What a sinister hour for the fatal ceremony. The strange fascination that that man's glance has over me... It's death, death!

SIR WILLIAM

(approaching his daughter)

Are you preparing to present yourself at the altar with your eyes swimming in tears?

ANNA

Father! Don't punish me so cruelly. I implore you again to let me escape from this marriage, the very thought of which casts me into terror. Don't deceive yourself: there can be no happiness for me in this marriage. Touching his hand freezes my blood. I'm not asking you to be Maxwell's wife. You love your Anna, right? I'll go into a convent. But don't marry me to that man. You'll repent of it. You don't want your daughter dead.

SIR WILLIAM

You're mad. Come, Dick

ANNA

My God! My God!

DICK THORN

Poor little thing.

SIR WILLIAM

I'm counting on you.

DICK THORN
(pulling his sword from its scabbard)
Suppose I were to kill him a second time? Think it over.

He leaves.

ANNA
My God, give me the strength…

FANNY
(outside)
Anna!

ANNA
(cocking an ear)
Did I hear my name?

FANNY
(outside)
Anna!

ANNA
Who's there?

FANNY
(outside)
Anna, open up, it's me, Fanny!

ANNA
(running to open)
Fanny!

Fanny enters, barely able to contain herself.

FANNY

At last!

ANNA

What's the matter with you? Where are you coming from?

FANNY

I was afraid I'd get here too late.

ANNA

Too late?

FANNY

I was afraid that this marriage—

ANNA

It's to take place at midnight.

FANNY

It makes me tremble.

ANNA

Why tremble to see me married?

FANNY

Am I capable of forgetting how much Maxwell loves you?

ANNA

Maxwell is sacrificing himself to my duty.

FANNY

Yes, you've imposed this sacrifice on him, and he's consented to it.

ANNA

Like a valiant and devoted heart.

FANNY

He's consented, but I haven't.

ANNA

Fanny...

FANNY

You've told him, "Forget me!" You didn't see his tears, his despair. You are still all of his life; you cannot be unaware of that. I swear to you that Maxwell will die if you become someone else's wife. Find a way to move your father.

ANNA

My father is one of those inflexible men that no force on Earth can move. I begged him; but he regards me as mad.

FANNY

Still, you mustn't become Lord Ruthven's wife! You mustn't!

ANNA

Fanny!

FANNY

My God! I feel ill! I am speaking to you of my brother's despair; you respond to me with talk of your obedience to your father's commands. But what about me?

ANNA

You?

FANNY

Yes. Don't you understand that this marriage is also breaking my heart?

ANNA

But you are Reginald's fiancée?

FANNY

But I love Lord Ruthven!

ANNA

That's impossible.

FANNY

How to convince you?... Ah, I know! You've taken comfort in the thought that Maxwell would never love another woman?

ANNA

That's true.

FANNY

Now suppose you imagined Maxwell in the arms of another woman?

ANNA

No!

FANNY

Well, as for me, I shiver thinking that Lord Ruthven is going to marry you. That idea drives me mad.

ANNA

You are jealous?

FANNY

Yes I am. I don't wish, do you hear, I don't want you to become his wife. Tell me again that you don't love him!

ANNA

But what about Reginald?

FANNY

Reginald? When I agreed to marry him, I hadn't seen Lord Ruthven yet... Anna, promise me you will reject this marriage. Promise me!

ANNA

Fanny! But how? I don't know how to answer you. Is there some way?

FANNY

Yes.

ANNA

Tell me what it is.

At that moment, Tom Platt enters.

TOM PLATT

Miss Anna…

FANNY

Come! Come with me! And the two of us will be saved.

ANNA

But…?

FANNY

Come with me, I tell you!

The two women leave together.

TOM PLATT

She didn't pay any attention to me, but I don't wish her ill for that. It's a trifle difficult to tell a woman that her intended won't be coming to the ceremony on account of him being dead, because Mr. Reginald shot him. I fell a little ill, but when I came to afterward, they were straightaway burying Lord Ruthven who, I don't blush to admit it, I do not enormously miss… He was a bit too slick for my tastes… My young master sees Miss Anna, he proposes marriage to her. He sees Betsy, he talks to her of… Well, he didn't propose marriage to her, not to Betsy… A great Lord who talks about sweet nothings, that's titillating. But today, he rests with a fine beautiful stone on his stomach. There's nothing that calms passion like a marble stone. Betsy's a flirt, I should scold her, but if she ever harkened to the blandishments of my former young master, Lord Ruthven, I'll…

Ruthven enters on these last words, hears them, and taps Tom Platt on the shoulder.

RUTHVEN

You'll do what, Tom?

TOM PLATT
(trembling)
That voice? It can't be!

RUTHVEN

Aren't you quite sure of your wife's devotion?

TOM PLATT

Him! Here! It's the Devil's work!
(to Ruthven)
When I say you, Milord, it's not you I meant…
(aside)
Ah, this makes my flesh crawl.

RUTHVEN

Why are you so surprised to see me?

TOM PLATT

I'm not surprised at all, Milord! Only… I thought… I was almost certain… Oh, everything's spinning!

RUTHVEN

A newlywed's joy, Master Tom. Quite understandable.
(tapping him on the shoulder in a friendly way)
But I'm a generous master. I forgive you.

TOM PLATT
(rubbing his shoulder)
That's firm. From the hand of a revenant, I would never have believed it.

RUTHVEN
(leaning on him)
A happy bumpkin, with such a charming wife. Admit it, you were jealous?

TOM: PLATT
(shivering)
Why, yes Milord, a little.

RUTHVEN

Are you cold?

Tom shakes his head.

RUTHVEN
Is everything ready for the ceremony?

TOM PLATT
(stammering)
Wh-what ce-ceremon-ny?

RUTHVEN
I didn't know you had a speech impediment. What ceremony? Tom! Was your marriage the only one? Didn't you think a little of mine?

TOM PLATT
Your... Your m-marr...iage?

RUTHVEN
Yes. Miss Anna is ready. I was... delayed.

TOM PLATT

Delayed… right.

RUTHVEN

Where's Sir William? Why this delay when I'm burning with impatience?

TOM PLATT:

Burning with impatience, right.

RUTHVEN

Heavens! I've got it! It's that stupid story from yesterday! That's why I find you here, all tongue-tied. This is a good thing too. You must understand the need for discretion?

TOM PLATT
(shivering)

I seem to no longer have a tongue, Milord.

RUTHVEN

Satan preserve you from it! Be mute or I'll kill you.

TOM PLATT

Yes, mute. Understood, Milord.

RUTHVEN

Breathe one word and you're a dead man.

TOM PLATT

A dead man, right, Milord,

RUTHVEN

I hear the wedding party; it's them. At last!

Sir William enters with Dick Thorn.

SIR WILLIAM
Everything's ready, Milord. We're waiting only for the bride.

RUTHVEN
Miss Anna is not with you, Sir William?

SIR WILLIAM
She's in the last act of dressing.

DICK THORN
(aside, looking at Ruthven)
He's quite pale for a man—still, his eyes are too bright for a revenant. I'm perplexed.

A woman, covered with a veil, enters from the room at the left.

SIR WILLIAM
Here's your bride, Lord Ruthven.

RUTHVEN
Finally, darling Anna, my wishes have outrun the hour. You will forgive my impatience, because it comes from the most sincere and passionate love.

SIR WILLIAM
(to Dick Thorn)
Anna's resigned to this marriage! Everything is going according to my desire.

DICK THORN
I bet he vanishes at the foot of the altar.

A sound of clocks is heard.

RUTHVEN
The chapel's ready. They're waiting for us. Come, my beautiful bride, come!

Sir William gives the woman his hand. Ruthven puts his arm into that of Dick Thorn, who shivers involuntarily.

RUTHVEN
Well, my valiant Captain, you still wish me ill with that furious thrust? That would be too rancorous.

DICK THORN
(aside)
I am perplexed. Decidedly, perplexed.

TOM PLATT
(following them)
Which of the two of us is the villain here? Him, or I who remain silent?

Everyone leaves. Then, Anna emerges from the room on the left.

ANNA
They've gone! What will become of Fanny, who has taken my place? How she loves him! Should I have consented? All my doubts evaporated before her prayers. I must not be troubled by her words anymore. But still, I can't help wondering, what will come of all this?

Maxwell enters from the rear.

MAXWELL

There's no one to tell me…
(seeing Anna)
Anna! (with a great shout of joy) Anna!

ANNA

Maxwell.
(aside)
What will he say when he learns the truth?

MAXWELL

You cannot know how your presence reassures me. The
terrible danger that I thought you were in…

ANNA

What danger?

MAXWELL

I shouldn't say anymore. You'd probably accuse me of
being mad.

ANNA

I don't understand you.

MAXWELL

Don't believe that I'm a stupid, jealous man. Now, your
father must listen to me, believe me.

ANNA

Believe you? What have you to tell him? What is so terrible about this marriage?

MAXWELL

It's certain death.

ANNA
(fearful)

Ah…

MAXWELL

Why be afraid? You're still free. I shall speak.

ANNA

It's too late.

MAXWELL

What is too late? This marriage won't take place.

We hear the sounds of clocks striking outside.

ANNA
(with a little scream)

It has taken place!

MAXWELL
(looking outside)

But you are here, with me, and Lord Ruthven…?

ANNA

Lord Ruthven is now her husband.

MAXWELL

Whose husband?

ANNA

She took my place.

MAXWELL

Who did?

ANNA

Fanny! Maxwell, this terrible and incredible accusation
you are making against Lord Ruthven...

MAXWELL

On my eternal salvation, it's all true, I swear it!

ANNA

My God! She must have known and sacrificed herself to
save me.

MAXWELL

But I sent her away.

ANNA

She came back to save me. Let's run, let's run away...

Sir William returns, with Dick Thorn.

ANNA
(recoiling)

Father!

SIR WILLIAM

Anna? You, here? I'm dreaming! But who did His Lordship marry then?

ANNA

She sacrificed herself to save me from a horrible death.

SIR WILLIAM

And what is Doctor Maxwell doing in my home?

ANNA

Ruthven is an infernal spirit.

SIR WILLIAM

What do you mean?

ANNA

If it were otherwise, would Fanny have come here to take the veil which should have been my shroud?

SIR WILLIAM

Unhappy child, what are you saying?

ANNA

I'm saying that if she dies, I will die too, because I'm the one he would have killed.

MAXWELL

But where is she? Where are they?

DICK THORN

In the bridal suite.

ANNA

The death chamber.

SIR WILLIAM

Anna! You can't mean…?

ANNA

Look me in the face, father. Am I mad? Heaven won't allow such a crime to be accomplished. Come!

SIR WILLIAM

Anna…

ANNA

Will you come!

Tom Platt enters and presents a letter to Sir William.

TOM PLATT

A letter from Lord Ruthven, sir.

SIR WILLIAM
(taking the letter)

A letter? For me?

ALL

Read it, read it!

SIR WILLIAM
(unfolding the letter)

God damn me if I don't feel their madness infecting me, too.
(reading)

"Sir William, I have enemies. Twice already, I've escaped their ambushes, but I'll surely perish the third time…"

ALL

Oh!

SIR WILLIAM
(continues reading)
"…if I don't leave at once, taking my newlywed wife with me."

ALL

Heavens!

SIR WILLIAM
(continues reading)
"Tell those who thought to have twice placed me in the tomb, that I laugh at their impotent weapons."

DICK THORN
(twisting his fist on his sword)

Impotent!

SIR WILLIAM
(continues reading)
"I'm leaving, and I shall greet the dawn of my resurrection on the bridge of the brig *Inferno* from where I defy their rage and their wrath."
(bemused)
What horrible mystery.

MAXWELL

On the bridge of the *Inferno*…

DICK THORN

Let's rush to the harbor.

We hear cannon shots in the distance.

ALL
(recoiling with fright)
He's gone to sea!

ANNA
Fanny! My sister lost forever.

MAXWELL
No. A few hours of night still remain.

DICK THORN
We must profit by them.

MAXWELL
We need a ship. And rowers. Strong men.

ANNA
Go! I will pray.

MAXWELL
Yes, pray, pray, dear Anna. Fanny's dying for my crime and your prayers must rise to God so that He'll permit me to save her!

CURTAIN

ACT V

Scene VII

The rear of the bridge of the *Inferno*. The poop deck is facing the audience. To the left and right are large stairways leading to it. In the middle of the stage, we see the main mast. In the rear, behind the mast, there is a door to the cabin. The ship's lantern is on the poop. It is night.

AT RISE, the ship's light shines into the darkness. Lord Ruthven, standing on the deck, scans the horizon. Sailors are leaning on ropes, also looking into the distance. A sailor armed with a telescope also scans the distance.

RUTHVEN
Well, those ships?

SAILOR
Those ships are pursuing us, Milord! They are steering towards us.

RUTHVEN:
Turn to the wind! We'll put distance between us and them most quickly that way.
                    (coming down the deck)
Maxwell arrived too late. Everything was over. But he convinced Sir William of my true nature. Ah, Doctor Maxwell, Anna is my prey. Her pure and virginal blood must consecrate the life that you restored in me. At this time, I defy you, I challenge you!

RUTHVEN (cont'd)

I understand your remorse, your desire for vengeance. You wish to annihilate your work. But despite all your efforts, I remain standing.

SAILOR

Milord! Milord!

RUTHVEN

What's wrong?

SAILOR

Despite the fog, their lights are getting brighter. They're getting closer.

RUTHVEN

Where are we?

SAILOR

In the open sea, but the wind's falling.

RUTHVEN

What, after all, do we care about these men? Aren't there enough of us to fight them?

SECOND SAILOR

But we've got no other arms than our axes.

RUTHVEN

An axe kills just as neatly as a musket ball. I've paid you well. They must not be allowed to board this ship.

SAILOR

The weather's darkening. There's a storm in the distance.

RUTHVEN

Hell is protecting me. Those who are pursuing me will be engulfed by the squall.

SAILOR

The wind is blowing only at intervals now. The sails are beating the mast. Your enemies are getting closer.

RUTHVEN

Put out the ship's light. That way, they'll proceed without direction.

ALL

Put out the ship's light!

SAILOR

But that will attract other perils to us…

RUTHVEN

I order it!

The lamp is extinguished.

SECOND SAILOR

No more wind! No more wind!

RUTHVEN

Blow, will you, cursed breeze! Swell the sails! Hurricane, unchain yourself—only for an hour. Carry us to the end of the world!

SAILOR

In a quarter of an hour, we will be boarded.

RUTHVEN

Go down into the hold. Watch through the port hole. Leave the helm, and leave the ship to her own designs.

THIRD SAILOR

Abandon the helm?

SAILOR

But what if the storm comes?

RUTHVEN

You'll resume your posts at my call. Go! Go!

The sailors leave.

RUTHVEN

The hour's approaching .I feel it. I divine it from the shivering of my entire being. If I have not poured into my veins the blood which gives me life before it comes, I'll have to return to the grave—and fear never to emerge again, except at night, and then only for an hour, forced to flee daylight and curse the Sun's rays, submitting completely to the laws of Hell. All the sufferings of the damned! Come on, vampire! Eternal existence is yours. Now is the moment when you must sacrifice your victim!

He goes to the cabin and opens the door.

RUTHVEN

Anna! Anna!

Fanny appears in the doorway.

FANNY

Who's calling me?

RUTHVEN

It is I—your husband! Your friend, your lover!

FANNY
(coming forward)
My God! Give me the courage. I'm afraid. I'm scared.

RUTHVEN

Why tremble like that? I love you, Anna. I love you with all the strength of my being. Didn't your father give you to me? Aren't you my life? My treasure? My happiness?

FANNY:

Your life!

RUTHVEN

Let a word escape from your lips which may make me believe you don't curse this marriage! Raise the veil which hides from me the features that I've only glimpsed and that I am burning to contemplate again. Let me read in your beautiful eyes all the love I have for you.

FANNY

Please leave me alone.

RUTHVEN

Are you holding it against me that I've torn you so abruptly from the embrace of your father? But aren't you with me? Me, who'll make your life so happy that you'll forget everything, father, family, country. I want to press you to my heart so that you can hear its beatings. It's to your lips that I must fasten, to make you understand all that my words fail to express when describing the love I feel for you.

FANNY
(moving away from him)
Leave me alone!

The storm scolds in the distance, some lightning ploughs through the clouds.

RUTHVEN

Anna! Anna!

FANNY

If dawn would only come.

RUTHVEN

Anna! Anna! I love you. Tear off this veil, I beg you. It makes me despair.

FANNY
(moving away)
And I tell you to leave me alone!

RUTHVEN

Ah, you shall not resist my entreaties! You are mine! I am your master! You will obey me. Tear off this veil!

The storm increases.

> FANNY

My God, why dawn won't come?

> RUTHVEN

If you won't obey I shall force you!

Fanny pulls a dagger from her breast and pushes her veil
aside.

> FANNY

Come closer, monster, if you dare!

> RUTHVEN

Ah, Fanny! Fanny!

> FANNY

Yes, Fanny, who took the place of your fiancée.

> RUTHVEN

And you would strike me?

> FANNY

One step and I'll plunge this dagger in your breast.

> RUTHVEN

Ah, ah, ah! She dares defy me!

> FANNY

Yes, I dare! I am still awaiting the hour when you must
return to the tomb. Die demon! Your prey escapes you in
the end! I am vengeance!

Lightning, thunder.

RUTHVEN

Your dagger's a woman's weapon—child's play. You are mine!

FANNY

One more step and I strike you down!

RUTHVEN

You are mine, I tell you. What do I care about my victim's identity if her blood revives mine. So you took Anna's place. Bad luck for you!

FANNY

A single scratch and you are lost. This blade is poisoned.

RUTHVEN

But don't you understand what I am! Don't you understand that I wish to live—that I need a life! I've got you there, under my glance. I will mesmerize you. Your dagger will fall from your hands. Your knees will bend. You will fall at my feet, vanquished.

Lightning flashes.

FANNY
(recoiling, terrified)
Those eyes, that voice! Ah, I'm scared. Maxwell! Maxwell!

She rushes up the stairway to the left, crosses the poop, and tries to go down the stairway at the right, all the while pursued by Ruthven. Turning round, she sees he's near her. She utters a scream and falls on the landing of the staircase, disheveled.

RUTHVEN

Superfluous screaming, utterly useless. See, you are trembling already. Terror paralyzes your arm. Your heart is going icy. I hold you in my power. My glance has met yours .You no longer see anything but me. I am your master!

Fanny, at the height of terror, drops her dagger and slips on the landing of the bridge. Then she gets up and flees again.

FANNY

Help! Help!

Ruthven leaps behind her and grabs her hand. She recoils half fainting.

RUTHVEN

Your soul is floating in forgetfulness. Your mind has lost its memory. You will love me. I demand it.

FANNY

No!

RUTHVEN

I demand it!

FANNY
(struggling)

No! No!

RUTHVEN

I demand it!

Thunderclap, lightning.

SAILORS
(offstage)
Milord! Milord! The enemy boats are boarding us. We are taken!

RUTHVEN

Ah!

Fanny collapses. Several sailors appear.

RUTHVEN
Let no one place his foot on the bridge of the ship!
(going to Fanny)
She is mine!

Maxwell and Reginald appear on the poop deck.

MAXWELL AND REGINALD
Not yet, she isn't!

RUTHVEN
I will kill you all. To me, sailors, to me!

We hear gunshots. Several sailors rush onto the poop deck and pursue Maxwell and Reginald who go down to the left.

Dick Thorn, sword in hand, appears with Sir William

and Tom Platt.

RUTHVEN
(unsheathing)
Ah! Bandit! I know your sword.

DICK THORN
You hear, Virginia? En garde!

They duel.

TOM PLATT
It's getting black as Hell.

SIR WILLIAM
Shoot! Shoot!

More gunshots.

MAXWELL
Sailors, Stop fighting for this monster! You are obeying a vampire!

ALL
A vampire!

TOM PLATT
It's true! He tried to vampirize my wife!

Recoiling, Ruthven escapes into the darkness. He grabs Fanny's body and rushes on to the poop deck.

ALL
Death to the vampire!

Reginald spots Ruthven in the light from a flash of lightning.

REGINALD

There he is!

ALL

Shoot! Shoot!

But Ruthven uses Fanny's body as a shield.

RUTHVEN

Go ahead and try shooting me—if you can!

ALL

Ah!

MAXWELL

My sister!

RUTHVEN

Doctor Maxwell! The hour has not yet struck and here's my victim! I win! Life Eternal is mine!

Suddenly, a lightning bolt flashes and strikes Ruthven who falls overboard. Fanny stands up, pale. disheveled, clinging to the ship's ropes.

REGINALD

Thank you God Almighty!

FANNY

Reginald! My love!

MAXWELL

God has indeed taken pity on us and has forgiven me!

All kneel.

MAXWELL

His thunderbolt has struck the monster, annihilating the work of Hell. Glory to God!

ALL

Glory to God!

Celebratory shooting. Freeze action.

CURTAIN

The Confession of Mary, Queen of Scots, Regarding Lord Ruthven

A small chapel. Mary enters and goes to her Confessor.
A bell tolls in the distance.

MARY
(to her Confessor)
I disliked him at first sight. It wasn't so much that he
wasn't good looking. I've liked men who were far less
attractive, but there was something about him, the hang
dog look of a constipated Puritan that revolted me. Nonetheless, I treated him politely, even affably. As a
Queen, I learned long ago… Actually, I was taught that,
just because one dislikes—or even detests—an individu-
al, it is no reason to be impolite or even cold. On the
contrary, such a person may be very useful as a pawn,
and one experiences no regret in sacrificing them, if
need be, for political reasons. And, in fact, I felt a little
guilty that I disliked him for no particular reason, so I
went out of my way to be gracious to him. But now, I
think, I should have treated him the way I really felt towards him, and perhaps, what happened might have been
avoided…
(she shrugs)
He thought I actually liked him. He became the most
assiduous courtier, and did everything he could to ingra-
tiate himself with me. That made me loathe him more,
but, paradoxically, I tried even harder not to show it.
Clearly, it gave him encouragement, and I believe he

actually fell in love with me. He didn't dare express himself openly, because, I doubt he could admit his passion, even to himself, the sniveling wretch. But the one thing I did not conceal was that, in every respect, I favored poor Rizzio more. Later, I learned that Ruthven had gone to my husband to excite his jealousy against Rizzio. That proved to be fertile ground. Ah, why was I so naive? In any event, I blame myself for being young, inexperienced and stupid. Darnley, my husband in those days, was proving increasingly worthless. Handsome he was, intelligent he was not. But that didn't stop him from being ambitious. "Why won't you let me be king,?" he would pester me. I replied, "If you want to be king, be a man first." Of course, that was beyond him. But it wasn't beyond him to be jealous, and he soon was conspiring to murder Rizzio, while Ruthven was urging him on. A jealous husband urged on by his would-be cuckolder against a man who was only my friend, nothing more.

CONFESSOR

Pardon, my Queen, but many say that Rizzio was indeed your lover.

MARY

I have to thank Lord Ruthven for that. But Rizzio was *not* my lover; he was only my friend—and that cost him his life. Poor Rizzio. Even after all these years, I feel like crying over it. Anyway, it went on like this for some time, until that fatal night... I was dining with Rizzio alone. First, my husband came in and sat beside me, and put his arm around me. I would have shaken him off, but the door suddenly burst open and Ruthven and his gang of cutthroats came in and demanded that Rizzio step outside with them...

In a TABLEAU, we see Ruthven and several lords appear. Darnley comes forward and hugs the Queen tightly, so she cannot intervene. Rizzio hides behind her as Ruthven tries to grab him. Rizzio grabs Mary's skirt tightly. Darnley pries Rizzio's fingers loose, and Ruthven and his friends pull him away from Mary and stab him repeatedly as Mary tries to protest, but Darnley holds her back. She still remonstrates with Ruthven and her husband and is clearly vilifying them both.

MARY
They thought I was helpless, but I was soon even with them. Bothwell killed Darnley, they say, but no one can prove it. Nor that I urged him to do it. But Ruthven... What to do about Ruthven? I decided that death was too good for him...

She stops and hesitates to go on.

CONFESSOR
(after a long silence)
What did you do?

MARY
They say I practice witchcraft. It's not true.
(she hesitates again and
finally takes the plunge)
But I know how to summon the Devil!

CONFESSOR
(aghast)
You summoned the Devil?

MARY
(slowly)
Yes, it's easy. They say in France that all you have to do is call him. He'll be there. So it was.

The Confessor steps back. In a second TABLEAU an eerie light focuses in a circle around Mary. The Devil enters. He is tall, elegantly dressed in the fashion of the day. He comes to the Queen and bows.

THE DEVIL
How may I help Your Majesty?

MARY
I demand a just punishment against an evil man.

THE DEVIL
Is not that within your power? Kill him—you have plenty who will do it for you.

MARY
That's not enough. I've dwelled on it for a long while.

THE DEVIL
And you think I can help?

MARY
Yes, I want justice for Rizzio.

THE DEVIL
Justice is not something people often associate with me. However, as for vengeance…

MARY

Vengeance, yes—but also justice of a special kind.

THE DEVIL

If you want justice, perhaps you've applied yourself to the wrong power .

He bows, and takes a step to leave.

MARY

Very well, yes, I admit, I want vengeance.

THE DEVIL

Of the cruelest kind?

MARY

Unspeakably cruel.

THE DEVIL

Then we are not wasting each other's time.

MARY

You know the one I hate?

THE DEVIL

Lord Ruthven, I presume?

MARY

Precisely.

THE DEVIL

I have a suggestion…

He whispers in Mary's ear. She listens, thinks about it,

then smiles.

MARY

That's admirable.

THE DEVIL

Devilishly clever—if I do say so rather immodestly.

MARY

You will do it?

THE DEVIL

First, we must summon him here.

MARY

How can I do that?

THE DEVIL

You brought me from Hell to this frigid place; it should
be a trifle easier.
(putting his hand on his forehead)
He is, I believe, having dinner at the moment. Summon
his soul.

MARY

Ruthven I summon your soul to appear before me and
the Devil.
(to the Devil)
Do you think that will work?

THE DEVIL

Absolutely.

A silence. Nothing happens.

MARY

It's not working.

THE DEVIL

Patience, my Queen.

Lord Ruthven appears, wearing a bib, with a fork in his hand and a drumstick in the other. He looks startled and angry.

RUTHVEN

Who wants me?

MARY

I do.

RUTHVEN

I'm not afraid of you. I say my prayers every day. I'm saved. I'm justified.

MARY

Maybe so, maybe not. But I intend that you suffer for what you did to Rizzio.

RUTHVEN
(summoning up his courage)

I am not afraid to die.

THE DEVIL

Oh, you'll not die at our hands, but we have a surprise for you.

MARY
You thirsted for Rizzio's blood.

RUTHVEN
Are we back to that? That's ancient history.

MARY
May you thirst for blood forever—and your progeny,
too!

RUTHVEN
(uneasily)
What's this thirst for blood stuff mean? What kind of a
curse, for it is a curse, isn't it?

Mary smiles.

MARY
Your children. You love them don't you?

RUTHVEN
You leave my children alone.

MARY
Oh, don't worry, I'm going to make them immortal.

RUTHVEN
(nervously)
What are you going to do to them?

MARY
They shall be vampires.

RUTHVEN
Excuse me, but what exactly is a vampire?

MARY
A vampire is an undead. It lives by sucking the blood of living persons and killing them.

RUTHVEN
Now look here!

MARY
And not only will they be vampires, but they will take special delight, as a culinary delicacy, in wallowing in the blood of their blood relatives, above all others. They will feed on your clan.

RUTHVEN
(suddenly frightened)
I beg you not to do this. The sin is mine, not theirs.

THE DEVIL
You've heard it before. The sin of the fathers is visited on the children.

RUTHVEN
Who the Devil are you? You mind your own business.

THE DEVIL
(bowing mockingly)
Devilry *is* my business.

MARY
How like you that, Lord Ruthven?

Ruthven tries to protest, but begins to choke and collapses. The lights dim as the TABLEAU ends. The Confessor returns.

MARY

They say he had a seizure over his dinner, and was sick-
a bed for weeks; he was never the same again.
(with satisfaction)
As for me, I can face my fate. I've revenged myself on
my worst enemies. The Devil has let me see the future.
It's not pleasant, but I have the courage to endure it. But
Ruthven cannot. And he's powerless to prevent it from
happening. No exorcism, no repentance, nothing will
alter his fate. The Damnation of the Ruthven's is complete.

CURTAIN

SF & FANTASY

Guy d'Armen. *Doc Ardan: The City of Gold and Lepers*
G.-J. Arnaud. *The Ice Company*
Aloysius Bertrand. *Gaspard de la Nuit*
Félix Bodin. *The Novel of the Future*
André Caroff. *The Terror of Madame Atomos*
Didier de Chousy. *Ignis*
C. I. Defontenay. *Star (Psi Cassiopeia)*
Charles Derennes. *The People of the Pole*
Harry Dickson. *The Heir of Dracula*
Jules Dornay. *Lord Ruthven Begins*
Sâr Dubnotal *vs. Jack the Ripper*
Alexandre Dumas. *The Return of Lord Ruthven*
J.-C. Dunyach. *The Night Orchid. The Thieves of Silence*
Henri Duvernois. *The Man Who Found Himself*
Henri Falk. *The Age of Lead*
Paul Féval. *Anne of the Isles. Knightshade. Revenants. Vampire City. The Vampire Countess. The Wandering Jew's Daughter*
Paul Féval, *fils. Felifax, the Tiger-Man*
Arnould Galopin. *Doctor Omega*
Nathalie Henneberg. *The Green Gods*
V. Hugo, Foucher & Meurice. *The Hunchback of Notre-Dame*
Michel Jeury. *Chronolysis*
O. Joncquel & Theo Varlet. *The Martian Epic*
Gérard Klein. *The Mote in Time's Eye*
Jean de La Hire. *Enter the Nyctalope. The Nyctalope on Mars. The Nyctalope vs. Lucifer*
André Laurie. *Spiridon*
G. Le Faure & H. de Graffigny. *The Extraordinary Adventures of a Russian Scientist Across the Solar System* (2 vols.)
Gustave Le Rouge. *The Vampires of Mars*
Jules Lermina. *Mysteryville. Panic in Paris. To-Ho and the Gold Destroyers*

Jean-Marc & Randy Lofficier. *Edgar Allan Poe on Mars. The Katrina Protocol. Pacifica. Robonocchio. Tales of the Shadowmen* (anthos.; 6 vols.)

Xavier Mauméjean. *The League of Heroes*

John-Antoine Nau. *Enemy Force*

Marie Nizet. *Captain Vampire*

C. Nodier, Beraud & Toussaint-Merle. *Frankenstein*

Henri de Parville. *An Inhabitant of the Planet Mars*

Polidori, C. Nodier, E. Scribe. *Lord Ruthven the Vampire*

P.-A. Ponson du Terrail. *The Vampire and the Devil's Son*

Maurice Renard. *The Blue Peril. Doctor Lerne. The Doctored Man . A Man Among the Microbes. The Master of Light*

Albert Robida. *The Adventures of Saturnin Farandoul. The Clock of the Centuries.*

J.-H. Rosny Aîné. *Helgvor of the Blue River. The Givreuse Enigma. The Mysterious Force. The Navigators of Space. Vamireh. The World of the Variants. The Young Vampire*

Brian Stableford. *The New Faust at the Tragicomique. Frankenstein and the Vampire Countess. The Shadow of Frankenstein. Sherlock Holmes & The Vampires of Eternity. The Stones of Camelot. The Wayward Muse.* (anthologist) *The Germans on Venus. News from the Moon*

Jacques Spitz. *The Eye of Purgatory*

Kurt Steiner. *Ortog*

Villiers de l'Isle-Adam. *The Scaffold. The Vampire Soul*

Philippe Ward. *Artahe*

Philippe Ward & Sylvie Miller. *The Song of Montségur*

MYSTERIES & THRILLERS

M. Allain & P. Souvestre. *The Daughter of Fantômas*

Anicet-Bourgeois, Lucien Dabril. *Rocambole*

A. Bisson & G. Livet. *Nick Carter vs. Fantômas*

V. Darlay & H. de Gorsse. *Lupin vs. Holmes: The Stage Play*

Paul Féval. *Gentlemen of the Night. John Devil. The Black Coats: The Cadet Gang. The Companions of the Treasure.*

Heart of Steel. The Invisible Weapon. The Parisian Jungle. 'Salem Street
Emile Gaboriau. *Monsieur Lecoq*
Steve Leadley. *Sherlock Holmes: The Circle of Blood*
Maurice Leblanc. *Arsène Lupin vs. Countess Cagliostro. Lupin vs. Holmes: The Blonde Phantom. The Hollow Needle.*
Gaston Leroux. *Chéri-Bibi. The Phantom of the Opera. Rouletabille & the Mystery of the Yellow Room*
William Patrick Maynard. *The Terror of Fu Manchu*
Frank J. Morlock. *Sherlock Holmes: The Grand Horizontals*
P. de Wattyne & Y. Walter. *Sherlock Holmes vs. Fantômas*
David White. *Fantômas in America*

SCREENPLAYS

Mike Baron. *The Iron Triangle*
Emma Bull & Will Shetterly. *Nightspeeder. War for the Oaks*
Gerry Conway & Roy Thomas. *Doc Dynamo*
Steve Englehart. *Majorca*
James Hudnall. *The Devastator*
Jean-Marc & Randy Lofficier. *Royal Flush*
J.-M. & R. Lofficier & Marc Agapit. *Despair*
Andrew Paquette. *Peripheral Vision*
R. Thomas, J. Hendler & L. Sprague de Camp. *Rivers of Time*

NON-FICTION

Stephen R. Bissette. *Blur 1-5. Green Mountain Cinema 1*
Win Scott Eckert. *Crossovers* (2 vols.)
Jean-Marc & Randy Lofficier. *Shadowmen* (2 vols.)
Randy Lofficier. *Over Here*

HEXAGON COMICS

Franco Frescura & Luciano Bernasconi. *Wampus 1*
Franco Frescura & Giorgio Trevisan. *CLASH*
 Luciano Bernasconi, Jean-Marc Lofficier & Juan Roncagliolo
Berger. *Phenix 1*
Claude Legrand, Jean-Marc Lofficier & Luciano Bernasconi.
Kabur 1
Franco Oneta. *Zembla 1*
Lina Buffolente, Jean-Marc Lofficier & Jean-Jacques Dzia-
lowski. *Stangers 1: Homicron*
Danilo Grossi. *Strangers 2: Jaydee*
Claude Legrand & Luciano Bernasconi. *Strangers 3: Starlock*

ART BOOKS

Jean-Pierre Normand. *Science Fiction Illustrations*
Raven Okeefe. *Raven's L'il Critters*
Randy Lofficier & Raven OKeefe. *If Your Possum Go Day-
light...*
Daniele Serra. *Illusions*

www.ingramcontent.com/pod-product-compliance
Lightning Source LLC
Chambersburg PA
CBHW020336260626
47156CB00004B/1548